CATALYST

Catalyst

THAMES RIVER PRESS
An imprint of Wimbledon Publishing Company Limited (WPC)
Another imprint of WPC is Anthem Press (www.anthempress.com)
First published in the United Kingdom in 2014 by
THAMES RIVER PRESS
75–76 Blackfriars Road
London SE1 8HA

www.thamesriverpress.com

Original title: *Aus den Fugen*
Author: Alain Claude Sulzer
© Verlag Galiani Berlin 2012
English translation © John Brownjohn 2014

A CIP record for this book is available from the British Library.

ISBN 978-1-78308-271-1
This title is also available as an ebook.
Thames River Press gratefully acknowledges the support for the
translation of this work from German to English by the Swiss Arts Council.

swiss arts council
prohelvetia

CATALYST

A Novel

ALAIN
CLAUDE SULZER

Translated by
John Brownjohn

Thames River Press

For my brother Francis, 1949–2010

I

Marek

Olsberg wasn't an especially orderly person, but he had kept a record of his performances for thirty years. He knew precisely what the point was: all that he wrote down in the old-fashioned, oilcloth-covered notebooks he had bought in London decades ago was a part of the life he shared with no one. It belonged to him alone. This bookkeeping would have been unnecessary, were its only purpose to record the various stages in his long and prestigious career. The staff at Heinrich & Brutus, the concert agency that had looked after him for twenty years, kept a faithful account of where and when he had appeared, what he had been scheduled to play, and what he had actually played. His encores were all they were uninformed about, because Olsberg always decided on them at short notice, often after the official programme ended, and he seldom notified them of his decisions after the event. The agency representatives generally attended his concerts when they took place at Carnegie Hall or Vienna's Musikvereinssaal. A phone call or an email would have sufficed to keep them apprised of every concert he'd given in recent years and, if necessary, to work out which sonata, étude or cycle he had already played in this city or that. No, it wasn't a question of avoiding repetitions. He enjoyed making his way through these numbers and letters like a man walking through a forest in which he knew every tree; numbers and letters that seemed far from as bald to his eyes as they would have to someone uninitiated or uninvolved. Olsberg was not uninvolved. It mattered to him whether he had played Mozart's KV No. 333

4

or Schubert's G major Sonata on June 12, 1979, or Beethoven's Diabelli Variations or Schumann's Carnaval on October 3, 1998, or whether he had given Bach's Jesu meine Freude, a Chopin nocturne, or one of Liszt's Mephisto Waltzes as an encore. It was one of his favorite morning occupations to leaf through his oilcloth notebooks and hum to himself in private, usually in a spacious, soundproof hotel room. All that was defined by these numerals and opus numbers flowed through his blood and aroused it just as the proximity of another person would have intoxicated him had anyone been there. But no one was.

Olsberg had lived alone for years now. He had long ago ceased to wonder whether the partners who had changed so often in his youth, becoming steadily rarer in the course of time, had suffered from his character or his way of life. Was there any difference? Had his lifestyle rubbed off on his character or his character shaped his lifestyle? He was a traveler on his own account. He was the thing on which his travels depended. It didn't trouble him to live out of a suitcase; he appreciated the fact that Astrid Maurer, the secretary who accompanied him everywhere, made all his arrangements. She was a selfless calendar. Marek Olsberg had been traveling the world unceasingly, every continent of it, since he was eight years old.

He was far more dependent on the quality of various Steinways and the qualifications of the piano tuners with whom he almost daily came into contact than he was on the favor of any lovers, some of whom had very soon turned out to be moody and insufferable individuals. He would have been lost without his pianos; without lovers he could live perfectly well. Concert grands and piano tuners were more to be relied on than any jealous and unpredictable lover. No impresario could afford to offer him a dubious Steinway — he spurned other pianos — or send along an incompetent tuner, whereas the lovers he'd had presented problems incapable of being solved by means of a few adjustments, whether minor or more radical. He knew this only too well, so it hadn't been detrimental when they became steadily rarer and eventually dried up altogether.

It had been up to them, not him, to beat their brains over why living with him had proved impossible in the long run. They were the ones who had wanted to share his life. He had often, with scant conviction, gone along with the idea, but it had always turned out the same way in the end. He tolerated a lot of things until it was all over. Then he sat down at the piano and played. That, as everyone knew, was the only place where no one was allowed to hassle him.

It was down to his fame, of course. Olsberg's eminence had initially dispelled the problems which he knew would sooner or later return via the back door. Nothing was more attractive than his fame and nothing more seductive than the affection and applause of the public, who cherished him. They loved him. They loved their Olsberg. But would they have loved him without his public? Could they go on loving a man from whom they would sooner or later demand back the love he could really only give his piano?

Olsberg was a figure of a man who, although he did not necessarily attract attention outside the concert hall, did so all the more as the moment for his appearances approached. He became a magnet whenever he emerged on to the platform. As soon as he started playing, he was the focal point of his listeners' world. All who had ever heard him in a concert hall agreed that hearing him live was quite different from merely listening to him on a CD. There was something unpredictable about his playing that defied precise definition. It was as if he had to conquer the piano like a mountain that offered him not the slightest technical resistance. He had to win and he always did; the harder the pieces, the more self-assured his mastery of them.

Anyone standing face to face with Olsberg could tell that he looked taller on the platform. Beneath the expensive materials in which he clothed himself, his figure seemed to suggest that he worked out regularly and maintained a healthy diet. Yet he exposed little of his body; his hands, nothing more. He had long remained extremely youthful in appearance; his age seemed to have congealed, and he now made a provocatively ageless impression. One would never have thought him on the verge of fifty. Few people knew that he was unmarried; apart from genuine groupies, no one in the classical concert world was interested in such details. His marital status could easily be checked on the Internet. What he regretted was his inability to limit his appearances to the minimum that other pianists found sufficient.

Olsberg hurried from one engagement to the next. He had been a child prodigy; everything had always fallen into his lap. In a few weeks' time he would turn fifty, and he didn't want to cross that threshold without making a decision. But he had no idea what form it would take or what its purpose could be. It was just an idea. Making a decision might also mean continuing to press on, not turning around.

On the flight from Tokyo to Frankfurt he took his notebook from the breast pocket of his jacket to remind himself of the programme he would be playing at Berlin's Philharmonie in three days' time. Two Scarlattis, the Samuel Barber, Beethoven's No. 29, and Schumann's Davidsbündler. The Federal President and the Mayor of Berlin would be there – as, no doubt, would be a few of his former lovers.

Esther and Thomas

"What's he playing?" he asked Esther, who was just applying some unobtrusive eyeshadow. The mauvy lilac shade would bring out the green of her eyes, which were already, or so she imagined, slightly obscured by sagging eyelids, with the result that they exerted less and less of their full effect. Grounds for despair, but not for throwing in the towel. She owed it to herself and those around her. Kohl and mascara. How was she to prevent herself from sooner or later getting hooded eyes like her mother and her mother's sisters? In her younger sister they were already more pronounced today than they had ever been in the case of her mother and her aunts. Would the genes skip a generation and spare her, or would they someday strike all the more mercilessly?

"Some Chopin, I think. And Beethoven. No idea. And something unknown. One can't know everything."

"No need to shout, I can hear you." He was sitting downstairs in front of the television, so she'd thought she needed to speak particularly loudly.

The lighting tonight would suit her, that was for sure. Subdued lighting prevailed in the Philharmonie. No glaring spotlights, not even near the platform, where she certainly wouldn't be sitting. Her friend Solveig had a season ticket for one of the side rows, hopefully with a view of Olsberg, tonight's soloist. Music without vision tended to bore her a trifle, not that she would ever have said so out loud.

There was no point in dwelling on it. What more could she have done to make herself look younger without going under the knife? That was the only way, everyone knew, but it was a road she would never go down. Her fear of surrendering herself to the skill of a surgeon, a person of whom she was just as scared as she would have been of a tipsy knife-thrower, was greater than that of someday being unable to look in a mirror without groaning and wanting to turn tail. What a disaster! What could be done about it? Like most women, she too had considered a hyaluronic acid injection after massages and thalassotherapy had proved not only expensive but ineffective. Thomas had long been pounding the treadmill in the basement, but not she. The effect of all these remedial measures was limited to the financial or physical effort you put into them, to expense or exhaustion, and they were considerable, even those that guaranteed to lose weight in your sleep, which they actually robbed you of. The rest was all wishful thinking, auto-suggestion, self-delusion. She had also considered botox, but believed that she could, from a long way off, recognize the frozen youthfulness of any woman who'd had herself mistreated with the stuff. So why run the risk of a partial paralysis for which the doctor took neither liability nor responsibility, only to have to hide yourself away for days and end up bearing only a distant resemblance to yourself? And in her case the treatment would be bound to have even more disastrous results.

Esther wasn't fashionably chic; she was a normal, well-organized married woman whose children had recently left home, yet she agonized about her outward appearance. She was no different from the women she despised, but she didn't despise herself. This had something to do with the fact that she and Thomas had a good marriage. A good marriage was one for which others envied you.

At fifty-four, she reflected at least once a day that she was heading for sixty. If not when getting out of bed, then certainly when standing unmade-up in front of the mirror while Thomas was already on his way to the hospital. There were countless opportunities to be confronted by her appearance during the day as well. Shop windows, elevators, escalators that glided past mirrored walls as they descended to the grocery department or ascended to the clothing department: places where she was tempted, respectively, by perfectly fattening foods and the perfectly fitting clothes she had long been unable to wear. She wasn't fat, but she was a tad on the plump side. She wasn't plain, but nobody turned to look at her save an occasional dark-skinned immigrant who was, she told herself, less intent on the satisfaction of his sexual desires than on marriage. She wouldn't return to 36, her original standard size, until she'd reached the end of the line and was lying in a hospital ward on the threshold of death.

She was flirtatious without meaning to be and felt old without being so. That preyed on her nerves. Thomas didn't have these problems. He might have others of which he never spoke because he couldn't do so without losing face, but vanity wasn't one of his character defects, as vices were called today. Or was it? At least she'd never had to bully him into showering once a day. He actually used the expensive deodorants she bought him, and the aftershaves and colognes in his bathroom emptied almost – but only almost – as fast as the twenty-year-old Aberlour malt in their USM sideboard, which she guessed was far more expensive than Calvin Klein's 'One'. She took as little interest in his drinks bills as he did in those for her shopping trips to Galeries Lafayette or KaDeWe.

Their children were no longer dependent on them except for money. Anne, their daughter, was in Munich studying psychology and this and that – the subjects for which her school-leaver's grades more than qualified her were forever changing. Gustav was in the army, but not as a dogface; he was training to be a systems analyst. Esther, who was happy enough if she didn't stumble over his job description, did not share Thomas's aversion to it. He found it embarrassing to mention Gustav's choice of profession in company, and she sometimes wondered if defying his father hadn't proved more of a challenge to Gustav than the ones that faced him in the army. Not that he would ever, he claimed, fire a gun in anger. Uniform suited Gustav, although a darker material would have gone better with the color of his hair. He felt good in it and was doing fine, he said often – just often enough to sound credible, Esther suspected. She and Thomas would never agree about their children. The arguments between father and son had been never-ending. Like his sister, Gustav had left school with brilliant grades and could have studied medicine at Heidelberg or political science at Constance, but he had chose to do otherwise. The army! He had opted for the unspeakable, for an outfit where one knew nobody, could exert no influence and derive no advantage. A professional soldier in the Bundeswehr – how absurd and old-fashioned. Esther sometimes had the feeling that Thomas would have preferred his son to disappear into the Foreign Legion for a year or two, eventually to return, purged, to the society he had once despised. But Gustav did not despise society. Unlike his father, he had not had to conform. He had always met the demands that were made on him.

Well, provided he didn't become embroiled in some business abroad and could operate his war machines at home, seated at a due distance at the computer. Esther, unlike Thomas, felt that all was well. The boy was alive, that was the main thing. She had no real idea of what he was studying and what he would sometime do for eight hours a day. Sit in front of a screen like everyone else, presumably, except that he would be doing it for the Fatherland. He still brought his dirty laundry home. She washed it and Bozica ironed and folded it more neatly than she had ever done. She could count herself lucky to have two healthy children who never caused her any problems. Anne did her own washing. Nine months ago she had bought – with her parents' money – her first washing machine. Munich was too far from Berlin.

"And what are you doing this evening?" she called downstairs as she donned her clip-on earrings, two turquoises set in silver. Inherited from her godmother and worn on special occasions only, they matched her eyes, though anyone facing her would have had to indulge in some ugly optical contortions to see this. Had Thomas heard her or not? The television was on low.

"Did you hear me?"

Having sharp ears, she thought she heard the fridge door close. Thomas was in the kitchen, anyway. Then came the unmistakable sound of a bottle of beer being opened, 1664 as usual. That was the answer. The clock struck a quarter to seven. She had to hurry, the concert began at eight. Thomas would make himself comfortable on the sofa in front of the television. That was the precise meaning of the opening of the beer bottle.

He came out of the kitchen and looked up. She had her head cocked and was still fiddling with her earlobe.

"Need any help?" he called. At that moment the clip snapped shut.

"It's okay. The fridge is full," she said unnecessarily, since he'd just seen that for himself, then turned and disappeared into the walk-in wardrobe where there now began those anxious moments during which she had to decide on the right evening wear out of dozens of dresses. She needed to be quick, which made it no easier but would perceptibly limit this time of indecision, which she was currently sharing with many other women. Thomas never went to concerts, Esther only rarely. He would have thrown on one of his suits – Kiton or Boss – without having to wonder if it was appropriate because he knew that it was. It would always go with white shirts, those being only kind he ever wore.

How did one dress for such an occasion? She knew that, naturally, but the longer she debated the more uncertain she became. It would probably have been the same if she'd been invited to the Federal Press Ball. She never was, of course, but she would certainly have allowed more time for consideration. Did they even hold one these days?

When she came down the stairs – only her shoes were missing – she looked more elegant than ever, and Thomas, who had turned to look at her from the sofa, was naturally unstinting in his praise. Sleeves rolled up, he was half sitting, half lying there with two beer bottles in front of him, one full, one empty, plus a plate of the day before yesterday's roast beef and some cheese from Maître Philippe. He really did look like that actor she'd recently seen on TV, the one whose name had just slipped her mind. No, much nicer than him, actually.

"Give Solveig my regards," he said, and she leant over the sofa and kissed him on the forehead from behind. At that very moment she quite unexpectedly lost all desire to leave the house. How much more satisfying it would have been not to have to go out but to stay here and stretch out on the sofa beside Thomas, eat some roast beef and cheese, drink a glass of Chablis or Sauternes, zap through the channels, and eventually go to bed early after dozing off in front of the screen because the programme was boring and the prospect of bed so alluring. Of bed and of something else, perhaps. Possibly a goodnight slice of foie gras. She adored foie gras, and it was seldom that there was none to hand in her fridge. Too late, though. She had agreed to go to the concert with Solveig, who possessed a season ticket, not only because Solveig's husband had left her but also because she appreciated Esther's company, even if she only sat beside her in silence.

Johannes

Johannes hung up and redialed, not on the landline this time but on his iPhone. It would probably be cheaper, given the exorbitant sums hotels still charged for phone calls even though the justification for them diminished with every year in which the number of cell phone owners increased.

He was wide awake with the wakefulness of jet lag, from which he suffered more and more acutely. He had spent three weeks in New York City working on a new campaign for West Landmarks and handling photo shoots with bitchy models and an unpredictable client who, after deciding to go with Johannes's agency, clearly proposed to reinvent the whole business. The shoots in Queens and Brooklyn had been discontinued after a few (expensive!) hours. Benjamin Pears, the client, had only just turned up – 'Hi, I'm Benny, these are my babes!' – when the atmosphere deteriorated and one of the half-starved, bloodless, ghoulishly made-up models keeled over. She was restored surprisingly quickly with vitamin injections and other expedients. After that they went to Brighton Beach and godforsaken Coney Island and the Lower East Side, the ugliest part. He'd forgotten the name of the street and the day of the week on which they spent until dusk making the rest of the girls, too, look like albinos and defending the set against inquisitive aborigines, with their earsplitting, curiously antiquated-looking ghetto blasters. He was pooped but he couldn't sleep.

He could definitely have used a cigarette now, but smoking had long been banned in Berlin hotels as well. Smoking was prohibited on all floors, not just this one. There were no smoking floors, no smoking rooms, no smoking areas. People had ended up in a place they would once have run from. But no one was running. Never did he hate his addiction more than at such moments, and never was his desire to succumb to it greater.

There was no balcony and the windows could not be opened. He had expected this before trying them, but he'd tried them just the same. There were handles, but what use were they if you couldn't pull them down?

Was it also prohibited to burn joss sticks? What if some religion demanded that its adherents observed that rule just as other religions prescribed unrolling a prayer mat and prostrating oneself in the direction of Mecca? He strove to concentrate but didn't know what on. What should he concentrate on if he couldn't think of anything else? He thought of smoke and joss sticks, fumes and cigarettes, and still he couldn't sleep.

In order to smoke he should have reconnoitered some place where smoking was permitted, but the only possibilities were the roof terrace and the sidewalk in front of the main entrance. He didn't even know if there really was a roof terrace and couldn't recall a sidewalk outside the hotel. In any case, he would have to leave the room to find out, and right now he hadn't the least desire to do so. He hadn't devoted any attention to the building when he left the taxi; it looked like all the hotels of his acquaintance, so he'd even ignored what might have differentiated it from others. There was always some difference.

Johannes disliked being on his own. He preferred the company of other people even if he couldn't endure them. They didn't upset him even if they bored him and made him restless. What upset him was being alone, the unpleasant condition that reminded him of his childhood. He fished a cigarette out of the pack, sniffed it, and stuck it between his lips. Tobacco! Fragrant crumbs! Gossamer-thin paper! That wasn't enough for him, though.

Why observe prohibitions when you could evade them with ease? With ease! That was precisely his job, evading things with ease. Blood, sweat, and toil had to be as little evident in the brilliant, amusing, original, genuine, imaginative, unrivaled, matchless, consummate product he was tasked with supplying as it was in what was advertised thereby and which sometimes claimed dead and wounded.

He got up and went into the bathroom, where he tugged one of the three towels off the rail and immersed it in the washbowl. Returning to the bedroom, he pulled off his moccasins, climbed on the bed – he nearly but not quite lost his balance – and clamped the wet towel to the smoke alarm from below. In this position it wasn't easy to light the cigarette between his lips with the lighter he now extracted from his right-hand pants pocket. The paper rustled, smoke rose into the air, he took his first drag. He dropped the lighter on the bed; now he had one hand free. He thought how nice it would be if a woman was there to give him a blow job. He thought of such things constantly. In the office, in planes, in taxis, with clients, during phone calls and conferences, and – of course – particularly when female employees were around. Emaciated models he found pathetic. Smoking was pleasant, salubrious, soothing, acceptable, and relatively cheap. Now he must take care not to make a false move that would set off the alarm after all. He took three hefty drags in quick succession.

He couldn't stub the cigarette out. Speed was of the essence. He waved the smoke away with the burning cigarette in his hand, then buried it in the wet hand towel and jumped off the bed. He could have broken a leg. Someone else might have done so, but Johannes didn't break a leg when he jumped off the bed. He kept himself fit. If you were fit, your age was almost irrelevant. He went into the bathroom. The alarm didn't go off. Maybe it wouldn't have gone off anyway, maybe the smoke alarm was just a dummy designed to deter people.

He called Karen, a former colleague from his time in Düsseldorf, but decided in the course of their halting conversation to restrict himself to asking how she was without telling her where he was at this moment. She couldn't have told, even if her phone possessed a display, because he wasn't calling on a land line. Karen was pregnant and spent nearly all the time talking about her husband. That was enough to dissuade him from asking if she was doing anything this evening. Of course she was. She was always doing something these days. Something about her voice was different than before. She summarized the end of her career as a stylist in two sentences so succinct as to render any further questions redundant. She wouldn't go back to her former profession, she said. She was happy. She felt sure she would want more children. And would have them.

He tried calling an old college friend and his widowed female cousin, but neither of them answered and he left no message.

He lay down on the bed, clasped his hands behind his head, and stared up at the ceiling. Then he remembered the email from the Berlin design office that worked for him from time to time. He had received it a day or two before leaving New York and had only skimmed it, paying it little more attention than he would to a spam. He accessed the email program on his iPhone, scrolled down until he found the message, and opened it. It was an invitation he would under other circumstances have tossed into the waste basket at the first opportunity. Two tickets for a concert at the Philharmonie had been left for him at the box office. He needn't even say if he wasn't going to use them; he was to regard the offer as an informal suggestion, not a burdensome obligation.

The longer he thought about it, the more vivid became the idea of luxuriating in billows of rich orchestral music, preferably Tchaikovsky, Bruckner, or Mahler, composers whose names he knew but whose symphonies he couldn't have told apart. He had never heard the Berlin Philharmonic live – who was their boss again? Abbado? He dredged his memory for the name. Rattle, of course. Renate, who knew about these things, had recently mentioned him. Several marriages. Interesting personality. A ladies' man. She was bound to have gotten that from Brigitte. Having decided to spend a cultural evening, he almost instantly fell asleep by way of a gentle, erotic fantasy. Oh yes, he still had to call Renate.

Sophie and Klara

It was months since she'd last seen her goddaughter. Would she have changed? Klara was seventeen. Sophie glanced impatiently at her watch, on the point of blowing her horn. Why wasn't Klara standing outside the front door at 6:30 p.m., as arranged? Why had she asked to be picked up at home? How much trouble was it for a seventeen-year-old girl to take a streetcar or a bus to the Philharmonie? After all, she wasn't chauffeured to school, was she? Sophie wouldn't have put anything past Klara's new father. Klara's new father was her avowed enemy.

Should she get out and ring the bell? At that moment a light went on in the hallway. Klara's mother was obviously not at home. Where was she? No, that was no concern of hers.

She hadn't set eyes on her sister since they'd lived in Zehlendorf, or not for five years. It was even longer since they'd spoken together, and all this after a weeks-long feud of which she still felt ashamed despite her conviction that she'd had no choice. Until then, Sophie had always believed herself incapable of losing her self-control. That quarrel seven years ago, which had alienated the two sisters, had taught her otherwise.

Klara wasn't to be drawn into these family hostilities, but it was probably impossible to conceal them from her completely. Sophie didn't know if they preyed on her mind. Why should they, given that she and her sister never spoke? Klara herself never mentioned them. She seemed to be interested in things quite other than family troubles, but Sophie had no idea what they were because she was no expert on the emotions of a pubescent girl. She didn't even know if Klara had attained puberty or was still in the thick of it. She certainly couldn't discuss this with the girl. Or was that what she expected of her godmother? Sophie was inexperienced in these things.

Just then Klara finally emerged from the house, and the sight of her banished the reproaches Sophie had just been leveling at her. Klara's face looked radiant, and not just because of the outside light that came on when she opened the front door. There was nobody standing behind her to see her off; either that, or they were taking care to remain invisible. She probably wasn't alone, but nobody wanted anything to do with Sophie. Klara wasn't warmly enough dressed.

"You should put on something warmer," Sophie told her, but Klara ignored this reproachful greeting, which sounded unfriendlier than Sophie felt. Although Klara couldn't have failed to hear the note of spinsterish reproof in her voice, she made no move, either to take offence or to go back into the house and fetch something warmer. Not wishing to give her sister – if she really was at home – any reason to feel surprised at her influence over Klara, Sophie forbore to insist. She wouldn't ask Klara where her mother was. Alma's name never crossed her lips!

"Are you okay? Not too cold?" she asked later, when they were already under way.

"I'm never cold," Klara replied.

"That's all right, then," said Sophie. Klara's health had ceased to be an issue.

"It's only September. May I open the window a bit?"

"What, now? Are you too warm?"

"It's stuffy."

She acquiesced. Klara lowered the window only an inch or two.

"Does it interest you at all? I mean, what Olsberg will be playing tonight?"

"Sure, why not?" Klara replied. She shrugged her shoulders indifferently but without hesitation, as if she'd given the matter some thought and discussed it with her girlfriends.

Then Sophie asked her about a subject she hadn't meant to raise. "Do you still play the piano?"

"Never touch it anymore."

"Pity," said Sophie.

"Yes, but I can't help it."

Sophie wished Klara's tone had been a little less decisive, less positive.

"That sounds final," she remarked, but Klara didn't reply. Probably because Sophie was right. Her decision was final because it wasn't a decision at all but the way of the world. She was growing up and exchanging her old interests, which had been talked into her by adults, for new ones. Sophie didn't know what the new ones were. At her age, probably boys. Or married, idolized, unattainable teachers?

She would have liked to counter the impression that she had inquired about Klara's musical progress merely because the piano had been a gift from herself, but she couldn't think how to do so without sounding reproachful. She could scarcely suppress her anger, she noticed, so it was perfect timing when a cat ran out in front of the car. She braked sharply.

"That was lucky," Klara exclaimed, loosening her seatbelt. "Nearly tripped the airbags, didn't it?"

She laughed, and Sophie said, "Phew, that poor cat."

She had first heard Olsberg play twenty years ago, here in Berlin, and she owned nearly all his recordings, she remarked a little later. It gratified her to note that her tone of voice was serene, as befitted an unmarried godmother taking her godchild out for the evening.

"Wow!" said Klara from the corner of the seat into which she had meantime shrunk as though intent on keeping her distance. The second "Wow!" that followed the first sounded less enthusiastic. Weary, more like.

Sophie almost inquired if she would rather have gone to another concert, but she didn't want to seem like the sharp-tongued spoilsport she would turn out to be if the evening remained as strained and humorless as it had been hitherto.

"We still have time for a quick bite, if you want," Sophie said in a conciliatory tone when the Philharmonie's yellow façade finally loomed up in the distance and they could start looking for a parking space. What material were those golden yellow panels made of? It wouldn't have cost her anything to ask Klara for her opinion. Why didn't she concede that the girl might have an opinion? After all, it was possible that she had learned what Sophie didn't know in school, but she preferred to go on treating her like a child.

Her search for a parking space above ground proved hopeless, as it always did when she took the car out at this hour. The concert hall's parking lot was already full, so she was compelled to use the underground multistory in Bellevuestrasse. It was probably too late to eat in any case.

In that case, just a glass of wine and a Diet Coke, or whatever else the girl might like.

Lorenz

Why had he dropped out of his math course, what about his chess, why hadn't he become a cabby or a bartender, why hadn't he thought better of it? Never having thought anything through, had he now, at the age of thirty-eight, reached the stage where no change was possible?

Yet again he cursed his decision to decide on nothing. What kind of a life was this? Insubstantial, free-and-easy drifting around, no reliable income, ever-changing places and clients, ever-changing, unpredictable employers, arbitrarily-paid work then no work at all for days on end, as if there never had been any, as if he'd been forgotten, as if there was no need to bear him in mind, as if he didn't exist at all, as if he was dispensable. Which was true enough.

He was as replaceable as any other semi-unemployed stand-in. Would he now be better off in Münster, where he'd grown up, than in Berlin? He wasn't needed in Münster either. The attribute he had long but not indefinitely been able to count on – his good looks – was slowly going the way of all physical attractiveness. What he still had, but didn't count for quite as much, were good manners, a self-assured demeanor, and the essential, carefully gauged balance between arrogance and subservience – all things that were somewhat more important in a party waiter than in one employed by a restaurant. Party waiter, what an expression! It summoned up images of a worn, greasy old suit that had been taken to a costumer's and forgotten about. He had never wanted to be a salaried employee, though. The very idea was a pain.

He looked in the mirror, then at his watch. That three-day beard had to go, likewise the stubble on the nape of his neck. Stray hairs were associated by sensitive women customers with food in which they had no business to be.

Still, there was one inestimable advantage to his insecure existence: the abnormal working hours. Lorenz liked nighttime and the hours when night was giving way to the pallor of dawn. Conversely, nothing repelled him more than the midday hours, which he escaped by lying in bed and sleeping to his heart's content, a party waiter not being needed in the mornings. As long as he could sleep away the mornings, all was still well with the world. He had never once been requested to work in the morning in all the eleven years he'd spent hiring out his services in this way, without ever having learned the profession. He was no breakfast waiter. The very thought! Breakfast waiters were the kind that climbed, unwashed, into the sweaty uniforms of which they had casually divested themselves the night before.

It was just after six now. While standing in front of the bathroom mirror he listened with half an ear to what the television was saying about stars, starlets, and certain events that had taken place, or at least been fabricated, in Hollywood. A place he used to dream of but had never visited and never would, save possibly on a package tour. He didn't kid himself.

The bathroom was small. The shower, washbowl, and toilet left little room for maneuver. He had to get to Potsdam by eight-thirty, the reception being scheduled for ten-thirty, so he still had time to spare. The first guests tended to turn up a quarter of an hour after the hosts and the last ones two hours later, usually just before the hosts would have liked to wind up the party and send the staff home. Part of the buffet would be set aside at least until the main attraction of the evening arrived. That could be toward midnight. It sometimes happened that the star was the last to appear.

Lorenz drew the shower curtain aside and showered as he always did: first warm verging on hot, then cold or ice cold depending on the time of year. He had sometimes masturbated while showering in the old days. He took care not to get his legs entangled in the wet, seashell-patterned shower curtain. He hated it when the moist plastic stuck to his body.

After drying off and swathing himself in his slightly less than immaculate white bathrobe, he went into the kitchen, the biggest room in his cramped apartment, and turned on the coffee machine. He caught himself staring into space – unthinkingly, not lost in thought – almost like his father, who had seldom left the house since he retired. Why did he live alone? Because it wasn't as much of an effort as a twosome? Why had he chosen this job? Because it was less of an effort than another? Why had he chucked college? Because it was too much of an effort? Always the same old questions to which there were no clear-cut answers. There was also another potential way of looking the truth in the face. It could be expressed by one plain, old-fashioned word: he was a failure. He harbored no illusions about himself, or at least, not many. As soon as he thought about his situation, it seemed untenable and hopeless.

Forbidding himself to stare like his father, he opened the refrigerator and, at six minutes to seven in the evening, took out what other people ate for breakfast: cornflakes, Nutella, honey, milk. He assembled everything on a tray and sat down in front of the television with it. Instead of staring into space he now stared at the screen as if looking into a void.

At seven, when the news began, he wondered what he'd so far seen aside from commercials; he couldn't remember a thing. Stock market report, weather forecast, a cartoon? There was nothing of importance, either in his own life or in that of other people. Was this the realization he suffered from? Was it this that reminded him of his father, that made him so like him? Lack of interest. No convulsion would ever floor him. He was a zombie devoid of relevant memories. He instantly forgot what passed him by.

This was his first job for nearly two weeks. Eleven days had elapsed as if he had breathed in and out once, coughed once, blinked twice – and this although he had often been assured that he performed his work to the supreme satisfaction of the firms that employed him and the customers he served.

Today was Friday, September 16. Little had been happening on weekdays for weeks now. Receptions were few and far between, and only young incomers threw parties on a grand scale – ones that weren't his scene. A lot of people refrained from trying to impress those who were financially worse off. Now they themselves weren't doing much better. People were drawing in their horns. Some were still doing very well, others very badly.

Standing in front of his wardrobe a quarter of an hour later, he decided quickly. The catering firm he was to work for had requested dark suits, white shirts, and bow ties. What else? Why these instructions? Didn't they know him? No, the girl on the phone had never set eyes on him, of course. There was little scope for decision in other respects: plain black socks, black shoes. He lifted his foot and discovered that the shoes he was wearing badly needed reheeling. The edges of the heels were dark, however, so no one would notice that they'd already been worn down.

He opened the window. The air smelled autumnal. The fall smelled like this in Münster, too, not that that meant anything. How did he look? He inspected himself in the mirror, tugged at his shirt cuffs until an inch of them protruded from the sleeves of his jacket, and turned on the spot, looking over his shoulder as he did so. You needed two large mirrors to be able to see yourself from the front and behind; he himself had only one. He still looked good, though no longer attractive enough to earn money with his looks as he had occasionally done as a photographic model, sometimes even for swimwear. He had missed the bus. Wrong agent, bad timing, not the right friends. None at all, in fact.

Before leaving the apartment he ate a chocolate truffle. That was all he would have for the rest of the night. He hadn't developed the bad habit of helping himself to other people's buffets or snacking on the half-finished plates of food that he or his colleagues had to clear away. Berlin kitchens tended to be spacious and the passages long enough to enable you to dig into any leftovers. He never did so.

He was wearing a light overcoat, but it wasn't cashmere. If he landed a few more jobs in the near future, which was unlikely, he would think about it. He turned out all the lights – there weren't many – and locked the door behind him. In the hallway he passed a young couple he had never seen before. He said good evening but they didn't respond. Like a lot of people in the building these days, they were probably vacationers who didn't live here at all. He curbed his annoyance at having said good evening to them and received no acknowledgment. Tonight, maybe he would find himself working with someone he hadn't seen for ages. After work, long after midnight, maybe they would go someplace for a beer and a sausage. An asthmatic dog was barking inside one of the apartments. It couldn't be faulted for lack of perseverance.

Claudius and Nico

Claudius had ordered the taxi for seven. It turned up five minutes late, but he curbed the caustic remark on the tip of his tongue. This evening would almost certainly provide him with some more opportunities to indulge in his penchant for unpleasant sideswipes. He was aware that they weren't always appreciated by those they were aimed at, Nico least of all.

He got in behind although the passenger seat was unoccupied. No plastic briefcase, no thermos flask, no grocery bag – nothing that nourished his prejudices except the smell. He avoided sitting in the passenger seat whenever possible. The last thing he wanted, when the time came, was to be sitting beside a cabby. Claudius was obsessed with the idea that he would someday die in a car crash. It wouldn't necessarily be a taxi, but in view of the way many cabbies drove here and the fact that he mostly used cabs to get around Berlin, he was pretty certain it would happen in a taxi. He unrealistically felt safer sitting behind even when he didn't do up his seat belt. He realized that this neurotic behavior was a phobia. On the other hand, what behavior *wasn't* pathological?

The vehicle's interior smelled the way trains used to smell, even in non-smoking compartments: stale cigarette smoke and wet anoraks. The cabby was around sixty, probably an alcoholic working on the side.

"Where to?"

Claudius told the man Nico's work address, 110 Schlossstrasse. As always when he was in a hurry, he intimated – less by a definite infusion of dialect than by his grouchy tone of voice – that he knew Berlin like the back of his hand and had no intention of being cheated. His West Berlin bus driver's tone was nonsense, of course, but it never failed to work.

Did they actually exist, taxi drivers who boosted their earnings by driving strangers to the area in circles? The cab was not equipped with a satnav. The driver must have been a regular dish in his youth, when that whitish hair was still blond. There was nothing worth mentioning about him now.

Dangling beneath the rear-view mirror was a plastic bone, presumably a mobile ashtray. They must be selling like hot cakes now that restrictions on smoking in public were steadily increasing. All that was needed to complete the olfactory illusion of a Berlin tenement house was a whiff of cabbage soup. He'd been instantly struck by this association as he got into the vehicle.

Yesterday it had been a Rasta with dull, matted hair who inveighed against gays; the week before a dark-eyed Iranian – a handsome, muscular man with shapely hands – who couldn't have praised the German capital highly enough before going on to speak of its one disadvantage: the multitude of security men whose sole function was to protect Jews, of whom there were definitely too many in Berlin. Claudius was used to all kinds of Berlin cabbies, so he had long ceased to be surprised by the way in which they blithely insulted people without entertaining the possibility that one of them might be sitting in their cab. Twice within a week Claudius had asked cabbies to pull up at once and fled without paying. His threat to notify their firm had been enough to silence them. It may have taught them a lesson for a day or two, but it was unlikely to have changed their views, in fact he had probably only reinforced their prejudices. One of them had undoubtedly tagged him as gay and the other as Jewish, and one of them was always right. Claudius himself was, most of the time.

The cabby driving him now had certainly grasped that Claudius was in a hurry because of his repeated, ostentatious glances at his watch. He wanted a glass of champagne and a bite to eat before the concert. He had recently spoken with Marek on the phone. They would not meet until after the concert. They had known each other for twenty years, almost as long as Claudius had been covering Europe for Heinrich & Brutus. The people in the Boston office were responsible for the United States and Asia. Their phone conversation had been brief and confined to essentials. The dissonance in the impersonal tone that prevailed between them was unmistakable.

He hated standing in line and knew that Nico hated doing so for him. "I'm not your maidservant, I'm not your slave, I'm not your lackey" – like the Goldberg Variations, the subject lent itself to ringing countless changes on the same theme, so he couldn't afford to ask him if he wanted peace and quiet. Although he dreaded having to enter the concert hall on an empty stomach, he forbore to ask the cabby to drive a bit faster, they were going fast enough as it was. He was a nervous wreck already.

Just as it did every third, fourth, or fifth cab ride at latest, no matter how long it took or what district he was driving through, it happened this time too. Just when he least expected it – in other words, when he should most have expected it – everything went black before his eyes and, as ever, he saw himself lying by the roadside, his mangled limbs encircled by inquisitive onlookers and a revolting, irresistibly widening pool of blood. Half deafened by wailing sirens, he was lifted on to a stretcher by gruff, foul-mouthed paramedics, slid into an ambulance, and driven away to the nerve-racking strains of the siren. A few moments before they reached the hospital, a narrow-chested pipsqueak of a doctor bent over him – the corpse – and ascertained that he was dead. His hand flopped lifelessly back on his stove-in chest when the doctor let go of it in disgust. He was dead, dead, dead. After that he lay for hours in a pitch-dark broom closet, one of those proverbial storage rooms mentioned in every hospital documentary, which he would have liked to be shown in a real hospital. Now and then the door was opened as if they wanted to check that he hadn't snuck off. No, no, he was still there. On one occasion the door slammed shut as soon as it was opened, accompanied by a woman's horrified cry. His mother! The next morning pale dawn light filtered through the dirty windows he was wheeled past. They maneuvered him along endless passages, then into a goods elevator, which descended into the basement, then into a cramped metal container. Opening a refrigerated drawer, they slid him in. It was like in a movie. Never for one moment did he lose consciousness. He tried to draw attention to himself, to shout, to knock, to move. No use. He tried to understand why no one during his lifetime had ever told him death was like this. That everything died except your ever-wakeful consciousness. That this would always be so. Never to be able to move, never to be able to emerge from this nightmare, alone in a refrigerated cabinet. Like a beetle in amber. In short, like Kafka's Gregor Samsa. Frozen with shock. Simultaneously dead and alive.

That was the reason why he had refrained from ever sitting behind a steering wheel. That he left to others. Others would ferry him across the Styx, strangers or friends to whom he entrusted himself because he had no choice. Or was he expected to travel by streetcar and subway? Was he to descend into Berlin's yucky nether regions, with their miasma of stale fat, and bury his nose in the moist armpits of half-naked cyclists? Never.

Once the horrific, long familiar images had faded less quickly than they had flashed through his mind, he opened his eyes again. The taxi was slowing down, a coincidence he hadn't been expecting. Surprisingly gently, without any screech of brakes and without pitching Claudius forward in his seat, the cabby pulled up outside the Saturn Building on busy Schlossstrasse.

It was almost miraculous but true: Nico was already waiting for him. The second miracle was that, even after eight hours' work, he looked stunning. Young and fresh-looking, tall and tanned. Stunning was the only word for it. How did he manage it? Claudius held the door open for him. Nico managed it by being young. Why couldn't you fuck in a Berlin cab, the way you could elsewhere?

Nico got in, and Claudius realized, even before he sat down, that he was in a bad mood. The first thing, therefore, was to cure it. Taciturn as he could be but probably wouldn't remain, Nico offered no clue to the reason for his ill humor, which didn't detract from his charms in the least — far from it, Claudius felt. The provocatively pouting lips remained shut. Nico probably hadn't taken any extra trouble with his appearance tonight, he always looked spruce in his own way. Did he know how handsome he was? Was he aware of his effect on people? To think what he could have made of his looks. It couldn't, however, be said that he was modestly content with his salesclerk's existence. Nico knew what he wanted but was incapable of grasping that not everything he wanted was possible.

Claudius put his hand on Nico's upper thigh and — like the taxi driver — set off for a central destination. But Nico pushed the hand away with a groan of annoyance, not lust. Annoyance at what?

"What's the matter?" The way Nico rolled his eyes sufficed to deter Claudius from insisting on an explanation. Pouty lips, fluttering eyelashes.

Claudius essayed a diversion. Knowing how much Nico idolized Olsberg, he repeated what he had mentioned several times in the last few days: that they would be seeing Olsberg in his dressing room after the concert.

"Astrid will get us in. Just us."

"Who's Astrid?"

"Why, his secretary."

"Oh, her."

Of course he had also mentioned Astrid Maurer, Marek's right-hand woman. Lithe, silent, and unpredictable, she circled Marek like an aggressive old cat. She traveled everywhere with him, though never in business class, accompanied him to every concert, on every journey, and had no private life — or at least, none worthy of the name. Ageless as Marek himself, she had lived for him alone for a dozen years, a small instrument on which he played without a sound.

"Exactly, her! If she wasn't well-disposed toward me, not even I, his agent, would get past her, let alone with anyone else in tow."

"I'm not just anyone."

Whoops.

"Okay, not just anyone."

"I'm hungry."

"Me too," said Claudius. He was already hoping to have skirted the worst of Nico's displeasure when Nico started all over again.

"Did you have a word with Heinrich?"

It went off like an indoor firework, but it didn't fizzle out. Although Claudius feigned incomprehension, he knew it wouldn't get him off the hook.

"About what?" he asked innocently.

He knew what Nico meant and Nico knew it.

"About me and my future."

"I don't discuss you and your future with anyone but you yourself. And then only if you want me to."

"I've absolutely no objection to you discussing my future with your boss. It's what I want. I want a different future, you know that. This isn't the first time I've told you."

But Claudius said nothing, wondering what that would achieve.

"So you haven't spoken with him?"

His silence hadn't helped to normalize the situation. The taxi driver seemed to be putting on speed. He also wanted to reach a conclusion.

"No, I haven't and I've no intention of doing so, I've told you that more than once."

"You never speak about me with anyone. Anyone would think you disown me. You do it although you're completely unaware of it. It's like I'm thin air, a nice little bonus, nothing more. The guy from Saturn, the guy from the record department who knows his stuff, but – "

"Nonsense. Nonsense!"

"No, it's not, you know I'm right. If you didn't disown me you could talk about me with your colleagues as if I really existed. But I don't exist, I'm thin air. Thin air!"

"Stop it."

The cabby didn't turn around. He didn't have to in order to hear every word and grasp what was going on: quite obviously, a spat between two gays. Ideal fodder for all the Rastas and Muslims in the world. Luckily, though, this cabby was a taciturn Berliner. They existed too, and Claudius was was grateful to him. However, Nico gave him no time to dwell on positive thoughts.

"You could talk about me like any other adult you know. Someone who knows something about music and business, who has made his mark in the classical section at Saturn in double-quick time, and is talented enough to make a start in your business. I'm not asking to be employed as an agent right away, I'm ready to start off in a small way, like I started off at Saturn, like I could in your outfit – "

"But we don't need anyone who'll start off even in a small way, I've told you that more than once."

"You tell me that every time, that's the problem. You told me that the first time, and the second, and the third, over and over."

"Why expect me to change my mind? I can't change it and I've no wish to."

"I deserve to do more than I'm doing today, can't you conceive of that?"

"You act like you're involved in a punitive expedition to Louisiana. Like little Manon."

"Don't make me laugh. I'd like to work with people I can look up to."

"You'd like to look up to me?"

"Sure, why not, if I had a reason to?"

"Oh come on, you can't be serious."

"Working at Saturn bores me stiff. I know I'm capable of more. I am, I know it, but I'm bored there and I'm sick of being bored."

"Coping with Russian sopranos, brainless tenors, and thin-lipped lady flautists is also boring."

"But at least they're alive. My CD's aren't. In your job there are conflicts to resolve, and I'd like to do that."

"How do you know you could? Maybe you're just imagining it. What have you studied? You've nothing to show but a commercial apprenticeship. We don't need any salesclerks. I'm afraid I can't help you."

"You don't want to, that's what it is. You don't want to help me. Of course you need salesmen! What are you, if not salesmen? You're nothing but!"

"Why don't you try your hand at modeling? You'd be ten times more successful and earn a hundred times more."

Half of those words had escaped his lips before he realized they were the last thing he should have said. It was unforgivable for them to have slipped out, but no matter how, no matter what, he'd uttered them.

What then exploded was no harmless indoor firework but a well-aimed hand grenade. Nico no longer looked as young and handsome when he flew off the handle.

"As a hustler, you mean?"

The grenade exploded.

"Stop the cab! Pull up at once!"

The grenade found its mark.

Nico's contorted face turned puce. This time the cabby braked neither slowly nor gently nor considerately. He swerved to the right and stamped on the brakes so hard, the taxi screeched to a halt beside a parked car. Nico desperately began to fumble in his pocket, meaning to pay his share, but either he was too nervous or his pants were too tight. He didn't mind making a fool of himself, but Claudius wasn't having it.

"Quit that! Stop it!"

Nico had never paid a taxi fare. Claudius didn't expect him to, it was absurd. He didn't want him to do so now, nor did he want him to get out. He wanted to restore the whole situation, and he felt pretty certain of succeeding this time too. It wouldn't be the first altercation that ended in an outburst — usually on Nico's part — and then in a reconciliation.

"Wait a moment," he told the cabby, and caught himself instinctively laying a hand on his shoulder. He realized only later that the man's loden green sweater felt just as he would have expected: repulsive, probably synthetic.

"Stay here. Stay here!"

"Get stuffed!" Nico snarled, and it was less this idiotic expression than the vehemence with which was uttered that shocked Claudius. Nico had his hand on the handle and eventually managed to open the door. Saying "Stay here!" was useless. "Hey, we were going to spend a nice evening together."

"We aren't going to spend any kind of evening together." On that note, Nico got out and slammed the door.

"Where are we?" he asked.

A stupid question. The cabby's reply was drowned by the roar of traffic he'd imported into the taxi by lowering his window. He was probably as embarrassed as Claudius by the scene he'd just witnessed. Why had he opened the window at all?

And now? Claudius sat rooted to the spot. Instead of running after Nico, he remained sitting on the back seat like an enchanted frog hoping that the princess would come back to release and forgive him. Forgive him for what? Had he underestimated Nico? He certainly hadn't expected him to show such determination, especially not this evening. That Nico would come back was as certain as it was that he would sooner or later start on again about wanting to work for Heinrich & Brutus. He needed Claudius, Claudius told himself. He would probably be waiting for him outside the Philharmonie. Almost certainly, in fact. He would somehow manage to get there first. If anyone could do it, Nico could. He would smile at him and all would be well, or almost. Well for the moment, well for the night on which he would introduce him to Marek Olsberg, whom Nico was eager to meet, whom he admired, whose recordings he owned, and with whom he might perhaps exchange a few words at the sponsors' party after the concert.

Astrid, later Verena Bentz

Astrid Maurer was as usual staying – though less grandly – in the same hotel as Olsberg, the Adlon Kempinski, but she hadn't yet seen her charge today. This was not exceptional, certainly not on a day that demanded Olsberg's entire concentration. At two p.m. precisely, before setting off for Potsdam, she drank a cup of tea. This was a long-standing habit to which she adhered whenever she could.

She sat in an armchair in the lobby, watching the comings and goings of hotel guests and their visitors. She herself felt unobserved.

Whenever possible, Marek Olsberg took not only breakfast but all other meals in his hotel room. However, he also felt at home among strangers who didn't know him. There were countless places thronged with people who had never seen the inside of a concert hall and to whom his name, if he had disclosed it, would have meant nothing. Neither local knowledge nor a secretary was essential to finding these secluded spots. If he wished to discuss something with her or sought her company, she was always there for him. It was probable that Olsberg valued her presence so greatly because she never made him feel she expected anything of him. She, too, could happily dispense with conversation. For the rest, she respected his mental divagations as an essential element of his work, which consisted primarily in concentration. She did not worry whether people thought they were mother and son, aunt and nephew, or even a couple, although it did not escape her that their eyes sometimes lingered on them.

Their relationship was purely professional, which was why they almost never spoke of personal matters. If ever Olsberg, who in contrast to her felt no obligation to observe unwritten rules, actually did so for once, she found it embarrassing because, when he became intimate, he was brutally frank. She tried to forget these fits of abrupt, unmerited familiarity as quickly as possible. He could rely on her discretion.

That a man like Olsberg needed someone at his disposal day and night on all five continents – yes, he had even performed in Cape Town, though only once – did not alter the fact that theirs was a working relationship. They still used the formal mode of address, and Astrid was thankful that he did not yield to the temptation to lift this bar between them, which obstructed the development of any hierarchical deformations. She attached more value to clear-cut relationships than he did.

What bound her to Olsberg was not secret love but undisguised and unreserved admiration. She did her utmost never to seem obtrusive. She didn't find this difficult because a more self-effacing person than Astrid Maurer could seldom have existed, and if she was proud of anything, it was that characteristic. Vanity was alien to her. Lipstick, eye shadow and other make-up she used as sparingly as if she were miserly. All she could not dispense with was hand cream, because her skin tended to be dry.

If Olsberg wished to see Astrid, she was there in a trice. It never took longer than a song without words, as Olsberg once remarked. Lately he'd been calling her only on her cellphone, something she had fiercely resisted at first. Olsberg had had to positively bully her into acquiring one. Anyone would think she hadn't been permanently available before, she complained.

She had tried within her modest limits to refuse, half-heartedly protesting and putting forward arguments she knew would leave Olsberg unconvinced. He had gotten it into his head and that was that. Her weapons were blunt and she was no real fighter – at least, not one that went to war with Olsberg, who had mastered not only Liszt's Twelve Transcendental Studies but also the art of persuading other people to do things that might conflict with their beliefs. If she fought, it was as a champion of his interests, not hers. Had she any interests of her own? Hadn't she renounced everything in order to serve Olsberg?

Olsberg had long ago become her exclusive and all-else-excluding passion, not that she would ever have breathed a word about this. What she had given up was not worth mentioning because it was offset by what she would never have obtained but for her devotion to the virtuoso: close proximity to a genius who – even when he was not performing – surprised and impressed her every day.

The cellphone he had prevailed on her to accept was a foolproof model, although he knew that Astrid Maurer easily got the hang of any gadget she was confronted with. Spurning a cellphone didn't betoken an inability to master its use in a very short time. Her initial reluctance stemmed not from incapacity or fear of technological innovations but was the expression of an irrational aversion. His secretary could do everything except pilot a plane, Olsberg had once told Maestro Masur and his Japanese wife, and Maestro Masur had given her one of the disturbing looks that were so at odds with his gentle nature, while his wife Tomoko gave an understanding, enigmatic smile. How did Olsberg know she couldn't do that too, the Maestro had retorted, and everyone – except Astrid, of course – had laughed heartily at this remark.

Olsberg had personally stored his number in her cellphone as speed-dial No. 2, so she didn't have to memorize it. Firmly depressing one key was sufficient. Astrid hadn't stored any more numbers, not even that of her sister in Könitz.

She never for a moment reflected that it was a special honor to be in possession of Olsberg's cellphone number. It simply went with the job, so she henceforth regarded the phone as a tool she could have dispensed with had not Olsberg considered it indispensable. She carried it at all times.

She received an above-average salary. Olsberg paid generously for her many and various qualities. She kept journalists and admirers at bay, not to mention members of his family, tax consultants, hotel managers, and composers. She would have been a match for any stalker. But for her commitment, Olsberg could not have led the life he led.

Astrid Maurer had obviously never been married and never spoke of personal matters. She was also paid not to have any firm opinion about things about which Olsberg himself had none, still less about those about which he did.

All that really frightened Astrid, who was fearless in other respects, were the migraine attacks that had regularly afflicted her since the age of thirty-four. She had in fact suffered her first bout very soon after Olsberg engaged her. The migraine, which seemed to cut her brain into thin slices with musical saws tuned to different pitches, always attacked her when least expected. Her initial attempt to conceal it from Olsberg had failed. He hadn't found it hard to tell she was in pain. He knew her weak point, the one she had no control over. It was possibly the only thing he, too, was powerless in the face of.

Astrid sat there for a quarter of an hour, no more, then the little teapot was empty. She had touched neither the sugar nor the milk nor the teaspoon. She was convinced that the combination of milk and sugar would inevitably bring on an attack. Why was she thinking of that at all? She didn't want to think of it because she believed the very thought of the worst that could happen to her would end by happening. Quickly, she went outside and got into one of the waiting taxis. The sunglasses she put on to protect herself from the driver's small talk enshrouded her in something unexpectedly mysterious. They were a pair she had recently bought at Saks Fifth Avenue.

Barely half an hour later, just after three as arranged, she rang the Potsdam patrons' doorbell. At least one half of the couple was expecting her. Verena Bentz and her husband were among the main sponsors of Olsberg's appearance at the Philharmonie. It would be his first recital in Berlin for a long time and probably the only one for a considerable time to come, so it was being given in the big concert hall. As Astrid knew, the Bentzes had contributed 10,000 euros toward the success of the evening, or nearly half of Olsberg's fee, which amounted to 28,000 euros. In view of the fortune he was reputed to be worth, this was a comparatively modest but helpful sum.

The lady of the house, who was wearing a flimsy, pale-colored dress, naturally had no need to point out that she would be wearing a different getup that evening. Verena Bentz was adept at adjusting to her surroundings. Astrid stared in fascination at her beehive coiffure.

Clearly aware of Astrid Maurer's important status, she did not, even by implication, treat Olsberg's secretary as an employee. She conducted her around all the rooms that would be available after the concert. She also showed her the kitchen and the two bathrooms on the ground floor, and asked if one of them should be reserved for Olsberg. Astrid said no. She did not breathe a word about the Steinway in the drawing room, loath even to broach the idea that Olsberg might be requested for a private encore. It went without saying that this would have been as lacking in taste as a request for an autograph or for intimate revelations.

No, there was nothing Olsberg did not eat because he ate everything with equal relish. They had already spoken about this on the phone, so Verena Bentz had also ordered caviar and oysters. She had initially considered adapting the buffet to the evening's German-American-Italian program, but this, on mature reflection, had struck her as a trifle vulgar.

Astrid Maurer praised the menu and, at the same time, intimated that even a thematic meal would certainly have met with Olsberg's tacit approval because he probably wouldn't have noticed the gastronomic link with the program. He attached no special importance to good food or good wine.

"Does he smoke?"

"Only rarely."

"Oh," said Verena Bentz, "then we should probably consider allowing smoking in the drawing room."

"No, I'm sure that won't be necessary. Herr Olsberg will prefer to smoke outside, if only out of consideration for the other guests."

Or only out of consideration for her? She suppressed the thought. She didn't want to think of it, but in thinking of it she believed she could feel a faint throb above her right temple. At once she turned her full attention to Verena Bentz, who proceeded to inform her that two waiters would be attending to the guests' welfare and that the catering service she had employed was one of the best in the city, if not *the* best. Astrid Maurer didn't doubt it.

In conclusion, she was handed the guest list, which read like Berlin's Who's Who. Leading politicians were represented by the mayor of Berlin and the secretaries-general of two major parties; the Federal President and his wife had announced their intention of attending, other things being equal; the directors of various cultural institutions insisted on exchanging a few words with Olsberg; numerous artists including the chief conductors of two orchestras, foremost among them Sir Simon and his enchanting wife, had also accepted; and the remaining guests were hand-picked friends and acquaintances of the couple plus such friends of Olsberg's as Astrid Maurer had informed the hostess of weeks earlier. Some eighty people in all. There had been almost no refusals.

Verena Bentz was expecting a worthy conclusion to a brilliant recital comprising Scarlatti, Beethoven's Hammerklavier Sonata, Schumann's Davidsbündler Dances, and a sonata by Samuel Barber. "It's bound to be a brilliant evening! I've only heard Marek Olsberg twice in my life, but both occasions were unforgettable. Once right at the beginning of his career with Justus Frantz in Hanover and two years ago at Carnegie Hall." It didn't escape Astrid that she stressed the last syllable of Carnegie Hall. Like a New Yorker.

Then they went out on to the terrace, and for the first time since Astrid had set foot in the property it almost took her breath away. In front of her lay a wonderful garden – a maze and forest, hideaway and park rolled up into one.

Verena Bentz glanced sideways at her with unconcealed and justified pride. "Yes, the garden is a work of art. I'd be happy if I could say I'd laid it out myself, but that wouldn't be true." She named a neighbor – "a fashion designer" – who had "occasionally" lent a hand himself. He had succeeded in remodeling what was already there to accord with his own ideas.

"He's not the person you may be thinking of. No, this man is young, almost unknown, and extremely talented. He dreamed, planned, and made drawings. Then he put his ideas into effect. He's one of the few people who possess the ability to revisit yesterday's dreams the following night. This creates a continuum of the unconscious. Simone de Beauvoir had that gift and other writers probably do too. It's an ability that's being lost in our digitalized age, one can imagine why. But that naturally wouldn't be enough on its own to create this. This is something special!"

So they both stood silently marveling at the result of the plans of her neighbor the designer, who would also, of course, be present tonight. "He loves music! He loves gardens! He loves the world, not as it is but as it would look if he could determine its appearance. We gave him the opportunity and we're grateful to him."

Then they strolled through the garden, which was really a miniature park, and Verena Bentz gave Astrid Maurer a description of what was indescribable unless one could actually see it, that is to say, the effect of the nocturnal lighting, which made the trees cast geometrical shadows. Only on closer inspection and because Frau Bentz pointed them out, Astrid spotted floodlights of various sizes located here and there and skilfully concealed from even the most observant eye. Would she, she wondered, like to pick up last night's dreams like a dropped glove? No, rather not, although… The second throb above her right temple brought her back to reality. She must quickly get back to the hotel and take an Allegro, even if she had to accept that – contrary to what the name of the drug suggested – the Frovatriptan would make her sleepy, not perky. Astrid always strove in vain to combat this annoying side effect, but it was less dramatic than letting the pain in. If only she'd had the tablets with her.

Anxious not to seem overly eager to leave, Astrid gratefully accepted Verena Bentz's offer to get her chauffeur to drive her back to the hotel.

Shortly before she left the house she was introduced to the housekeeper, who clearly had a firm grip on the domestic reins. Her manner was condescending and inscrutable, and she seemed devoid of respect even for her employer.

"Till tonight," said Verena Bentz. Astrid nodded although she felt almost certain the migraine would have caught up to her long before that, preventing her from being able to admire the nocturnal lighting. The housekeeper was standing behind Verena Bentz, staring past the two women with a face like stone.

Bettina, alias Marina

Marina, whose real name was Bettina, her parents having christened her after a celebrated lady novelist of whom, to her father's great sorrow, she hadn't read a single line (she knew only that the author in question was Bettina von Arnim), was counting on a peaceful, relaxed evening when the phone rang and jolted her out of her dreams of the long journey she would have undertaken if everything had been different. Galapagos, the Seychelles, the Maldives. Those were places she didn't know and would with a fair degree of certainty, unless some miracle occurred, never know. She was lying half-undressed on the bed, her open handbag beside her. On the bedside table were a litre bottle of Diet Coke and a tin of salted peanuts. Sundays had often bored her as a child. She had complained of them to her parents, but to no avail. These days she enjoyed the luxury of doing nothing, not that she could be said to overexert herself even working.

Because he was considered honest and respectable, they had given Marina's cellphone number to the client she was about to speak with. They had allowed him to contact her direct because he was obviously known to them.

Not expecting any personal calls on her business cellphone, she assumed the tone of voice expected of her. She didn't find it difficult, but it was hard to explain how she did it. It always worked equally well, morning or afternoon, evening or night. She spoke softly but not too softly, caressingly but not too caressingly, a little lower than usual but not too low. Her voice was quite subdued, with seemingly random vocal stresses.

"Hello, Marina speaking." That was how she answered calls on her business cellphone. Her father would have approved, but she didn't keep in touch with him or her mother and hadn't done so for years.

"Who's calling?"

She felt in her handbag and mouthed a name that didn't escape her lips. She thought it but didn't utter it.

Perhaps her voice worked so well because she imagined silk and velvet, wood and stone, fire and water vibrating on her vocal chords.

She tried not to form a picture of him, but his voice made it hard for her to resist that impulse. He certainly wasn't young, but not old either, and was probably well-off and successful.

The client's first name was Johannes. He didn't divulge his surname, not that that mattered. He tried not to sound too business-like but only half succeeded. He knew what he wanted. It wasn't the first time he had enlisted the services of Berlin Escort Services, the concern Marina worked for. He said he'd arrived from New York a few hours ago – he lived elsewhere but didn't say where – and met with a client – he was in advertising. He was flying on tomorrow and happened to have two tickets for tonight's concert at the Philharmonie. He was probably married like most of them. Nothing out of the ordinary, then. Nothing that concerned her in any way.

"Are you fond of music?"

She said yes although music meant little to her. Like so many things in her life, this might be attributable to her father, who had tried to impress on her, even as a child, how important it was to listen to music. She had abandoned the piano after only a few lessons. Her mother had made no comment on this. The piano – an heirloom, not acquired especially for her – was probably still standing in her parents' living room. She herself lived without music. All she owned was a television set and a small radio, not a stereo system.

"Yes, I like music."

"It's all the same if you don't, we'll just have a nice evening together. Would you like something to eat first?" He alternated easily between the formal and informal modes of address. She wasn't hungry.

"Only a snack, if at all." They arranged to meet at seven at his hotel.

"You're welcome to wake me if I've fallen asleep." He gave a little laugh and told her his room number. She made a mental note of it. She was naturally familiar with the Westin Grand.

She would turn up a quarter of an hour before the appointed time and call him from reception. No sex without socially acceptable foreplay.

"My name is Melzer."

She stared into space for a moment, thinking. "Mine's Marina," she replied, "not that it matters."

"What color?"

"I'm sorry?" she said in surprise.

"Hair color, not skin color. Sorry."

She described the color of her tinting as best she could. Only she knew the true color, which was mouse. She could have mentioned some further characteristics, but Melzer cut her short.

"Don't give everything away, I'm a curious man by nature. I rely on you and your firm. In return, you can depend on me."

"By all means," she said, trying not to sound too unequivocal, too naughty, too vulgar or banal. He'd said man, not person.

He hung up first. She sat there for a while, no more inactive than usual. "Amadou," she thought, again without uttering the name aloud.

Then she called the office to register the date. She notified the time at which she would get to the Westin Grand but couldn't say how long the date would last, then listed the salient features of the rendezvous: first a meal, then the Philharmonie, or: first the Philharmonie, then a meal. And then? The hotel? Certainly until midnight, if not beyond. She would keep the office informed by SMS.

Melzer was a long-established, generous client, said the secretary Marina knew only by voice. "He doesn't come here often, though." Either Berlin wasn't important to Melzer's work, or he visited it with a companion on other occasions, or he wasn't always as in need of company.

"Know what he looks like?"

"Not a clue. Like me to ask his last date?"

"No, no need. I'll see him soon enough."

"Soon is never too late."

Marina used the time available to her to draw a bath and make the essential preparations a man expected of a well-paid evening: face pack, nails (filing, painting, polishing), makeup, perfume. The whole, slow, meticulous program.

She spent no longer than ten minutes lying in a moderately hot bath. The beautician had advised against spending an excessive length of time, either in the bath or in the tanning studio. Not only for health reasons but also because more and more men preferred women who were less tanned than their wrinkled wives. They deserved something less vulgar than what awaited them at home.

Marina was satisfied with herself. There were more irksome things than going to a concert with a client. Better to the Philharmonie, where she could shut her eyes, than accompanying some chartered accountant or Swiss tourist to the Ständige Vertretung tavern, which certain people still regarded as a tourist attraction not to be missed at any price.

Claudius without Nico

For all his outward self-deprecation, which was insufficient to conceal his innate arrogance, Claudius was in his heart of hearts convinced, not only that he was unique but also that he was universally loved regardless of how he conducted himself toward his fellow men. In order to preserve his self-esteem, he secretly believed that they were prepared to forgive him any vile behavior. The fact that he had few friends notwithstanding did not worry him particularly because he felt convinced that he alone determined how many friends he did or didn't want.

That he had obviously miscalculated on this occasion began to dawn on him when the taxi pulled up outside the Philharmonie as gently as anyone could have wished. There wasn't a sign of Nico. Although some of the men standing around sipping glasses of white wine might have been a sight for sore eyes and a match for Nico in many respects, none could replace him. Not yet. Besides, the overwhelming majority of them were accompanied by pretty women.

But Claudius didn't abandon hope. He paid the cabby, got out, and looked around. He went to the box office where Nico, if he'd been there, would have had to wait for Claudius because the latter was in possession of both tickets, which he now produced. They didn't have the power to conjure him up.

There were masses of people there too, some of them fleeting acquaintances whose names he hadn't made a note of, but Nico wasn't among them. Claudius looked at his watch. Half past seven. He had just half an hour in which, in normal circumstances, he would have drunk a glass of champagne, possibly two. That he would tonight clink glasses with Nico – let alone have a bite to eat – seemed less and less likely with every passing minute. His stomach was rumbling. His incipient queasiness had nothing, he suspected, to do with the fact that he was hungry. It was the physiological alarm bell rung by a disappointment he couldn't suppress. He shifted from leg to leg, walked up and down in front of the big windows, paused before one of the portholes inspired by the architect's childhood visits to the seaside, and covertly kept watch for Nico through the glass. The humiliation of waiting was driving him mad, but there was no room for madness in this place. Claudius would continue to keep watch as long as possible, but every passing minute diminished his hopes. They peeled off layer by layer.

He decided on the extreme measure of calling Nico and apologizing, of lying if necessary and holding out the hope of a job of some kind with Heinrich & Brutus. Just as long as he came back. At once. He dialed the number. He had hesitated for so long only because he had expected to hear precisely what he did now. Not Nico's intemperate voice but the bland tones of the anonymous voicemail announcement. As he was closing his cellphone he bumped into a woman whose powerful perfume reminded him that the outside world existed too. They both apologized and the woman turned and hurried off to the cloakroom.

He gave Nico another twelve minutes. Nine. Seven. Six. Three. But the countdown proved a washout, like everything else on this godforsaken evening. Anyone watching Claudius would have seen a somewhat thickset (he wouldn't have described himself thus, of course), unobtrusively dressed man of around fifty who kept casting impatient glances at his watch. Ten minutes before the recital was due to begin the solitary concertgoer crossed the barrier that separated him from Nico and all the other people who were still outside. While the man on the door was checking his ticket, Claudius gave a last look around for Nico. He wasn't there. There was no going back. He wouldn't come now. Claudius put the second ticket into the usher's hand. "For a young man named Nico, in case he turns up after all." A last faint glimmer of hope. The man nodded and slipped the ticket into his breast pocket.

He could have bellowed with rage when the lights in the auditorium went down, infuriated by the thought that he would be unable to introduce his catch to Olsberg. How satisfying it would have been to show Marek, with whom he had been so in love and who had jilted him, that life went on even without him. And how! And with such a looker!

Marek and Astrid, Dr. Hiller and His Assistant

The day before the concert, Marek Olsberg and his secretary had taken a taxi to the Philharmonie. A few days earlier – from Tokyo – Astrid Maurer had called to fix an appointment with the piano tuner. Dr. Hiller and his assistant were waiting for them at the stage door. Astrid had seen to it that this meeting was as informal as possible. Marek did not wish to see the manager or any other official person that might distract him from his first priority. The night of the concert would be soon enough to deal with everything else – words of welcome, best wishes, and so on. The artistic production manager, with whom Astrid had arranged the meeting, had assured her that Olsberg could rely on the management's consideration.

Astrid did not notice that Hiller, who wore dark glasses, was blind until he greeted her – after Olsberg as usual – with a handshake that missed her right hand by only a hairbreadth. There was a moment of perplexity, no more. No allusion to it and no change of expression.

Hiller's manner toward Olsberg was neither constrained nor overly self-assured. He made a relaxed and amiable impression. That he was first-class at his job was beyond doubt, but he wasn't a man of many words.

He had been noticeably at pains to moderate the pressure of his handshake, which was doubtless naturally and occupationally more robust. He wished to spare Olsberg's hand, a courtesy taught him by daily dealings with the world's leading pianists. Attending to pianos required a great deal of strength, whereas looking after pianists called for sensitivity and restraint. Olsberg had heard of tuners who had been harshly reprimanded for failing in this respect by pianists less eminent than himself.

In these surroundings, blind Dr Hiller moved so briskly that the disability that had presumably rendered his hearing exceptionally sharp was not noticeable in the least. Without the aid of a stick, though closely escorted by his assistant, he followed the others downstairs to the basement. There, beyond a heavy iron door, were situated the piano store and the big elevator with which selected instruments could be conveyed straight to the concert platform. There was nothing tentative or uncertain about Hiller's movements; on the contrary, they seemed almost impatiently decisive, as though he had no time to waste on trifles. Not he but his assistant had opened the door and turned the lights on.

"Please go in, look around and select the instrument that appeals to you. And please don't feel pressured in any way," Hiller added after a brief pause. There was plenty of time and no concert scheduled for tonight.

Because Olsberg could not remember which piano he had played on the last time he performed in Berlin – he did not make a note of such details in his notebooks – he considered it essential to try out all the instruments that might suit him. Even if he had made a note of the instrument, his curiosity about the suitability of a newly acquired piano would have outweighed his faith in a personal experience three years old. It was always possible that something more persuasive had come along.

Since he intimated that he preferred an accommodating instrument, in other words, not one of those rather refractory pianos Brendel had always favored, at least three of the luxury liners parked down there could be eliminated at a stroke.

Only Schumannn would have suited the Fazioli, whose slim, elegant tone Olsberg would have preferred to that of the more powerful, majestic Steinway. Since he had long ago decided to play exclusively on Steinways in public – as opposed to the studio – he ruled it out. Hiller seemed to know this.

At all events, a hint was sufficient for him to recall Olsberg's preferences, should that be at all necessary.

"What do you think?"

"I'm thinking of precisely four that should suit you," Hiller replied.

Had they met before? Olsberg felt sure he would have remembered him. Hiller was a handsome man who titillated an instinct he knew he possessed but did not cherish because it had hitherto brought him more trouble than joy: the instinctive wish to protect one in need of protection. Hiller's blindness did not detract in least from his good looks; on the contrary, it enhanced his charm. In a sense, it got the better of his disability.

Hiller issued instructions to his assistant, who never left his side even now. He addressed him only by his first name, Boris. Boris, who looked more Latin than Slav, removed the padded dust covers from the four Steinway D candidates, lifted the heavy tops, and fixed them with the props, but it was Hiller who raised the keyboard lids.

Olsberg at once sat down at the first piano and, without a moment's hesitation, played the opening bars of Liszt's Hungarian Rhapsody No. 15, which would answer all of the questions he felt needed answering. They would reveal the merits and shortcomings of the instrument in the shortest possible time. It was not a question of finding fault but of discovering a correspondence between his ideals and the actual circumstances. He soon came to an unsatisfactory conclusion. The brilliant upper register failed to obscure the fact that the lower register, whose warmth had initially flattered the ear, sounded woolly and overly resonant.

Impassively and without a word, he sat down at the next open piano. Meanwhile, Astrid was regarding Hiller with undisguised curiosity. She had had a blind uncle who had year in, year out, toured country villages with his wife and two heavy suitcases selling household products, mainly brushes and cleaning materials, to housewives whom they knew from previous visits and who always took pity on them because they themselves were spared such a fate. Their pity was greater than their annoyance at being hassled.

But this man, who reminded her of her late uncle and the wife who was entirely overshadowed by him, had nothing in common with him except an inability to see. And in his case even blindness differed from the distressing picture presented by her uncle and his meek little wife.

By now Olsberg was seated at the third piano, and that one, she knew, would appeal to him. She didn't pride herself on being right, but she was proud of her acoustic sensitivity, which increased with every one of these sessions. The second Steinway had been strident in the treble and rather uneasy in the bass, which meant that the registers had sounded somewhat disproportionate in certain chords, whereas the registers of the instrument on which Liszt's test piece was now ringing out sounded perfectly balanced, or at least, just as Olsberg liked them. He broke off abruptly, almost brutally, and stood up. Turning to Hiller, he was about to say something when the latter took the words out of his mouth. "It has to be that one, doesn't it?" Olsberg, who wasn't easily disconcerted, looked surprised. He nodded, then said, "Yes, this is the one." He naturally didn't succumb to the urge to stroke Hiller's head, but he felt it all too distinctly. Like most people, he had never had sex with a blind person. For the first time ever, the desire to do so did not seem alien to him.

It had not been necessary to undertake the laborious task of voicing the piano by perforating the felts to make them lighter and softening the tone as a whole – a job which the assistant would surely have carried out under the supervision of his blind superior – because Marek Olsberg had found the right piano. He said to Hiller what he always said at such moments:

"My mind's made up. I'm sure this piano will withstand the treatment."

Dr Hiller smiled a private smile, like a Chinese. He inclined his head and said, "I'm quite certain it will."

Esther and Solveig

"What do you think of my new hairdo?" Solveig asked, and Esther just managed – or so she thought, at least – to disguise the fact that she had failed to notice how much fuller Solveig's thinning hair had become. Miraculous! My God, she thought, how incredible, she'd finally had some hair attached to her own. Real hair. Hair thickening. An extension. All those terms shot through her head at that moment. She herself hadn't so far been compelled to resort to this method because her hair was naturally thick.

The reason she hadn't noticed the change in Solveig earlier was that she'd retained her usual hair color, bleached with dark strands, which everyone had long been used to including Jürgen, the husband who had left her – quite out of the blue, she claimed the way all women do – for a thoroughly unoriginal reason: a young woman. For the sake of this young woman whose name all of Solveig's friends and acquaintances had tacitly agreed not to mention – no one seemed to know it, and it was never uttered – he had been prepared to leave Solveig quite quickly. Quick as a flash, to be more precise, as if he'd been planning it for months. And for good, it seemed. For good? Although they had no children. Despite their long years of marriage. Because of their long years of marriage. Because of their childlessness, which suddenly seemed to concern him. Or despite their childlessness. Whichever. He clearly hadn't found it hard. Solveig was naturally suffering all the more from the loss of her husband, her status, her self-esteem.

"Yes, I think it's great, really great," Esther said enthusiastically. The word "extension" was on the tip of Solveig's tongue, but she said it first.

"You know about them?"

"Yes, of course."

"Ever tried one yourself?"

Esther shook her head. No need. She didn't say so, Solveig knew it.

A stranger to laughter in recent months, Solveig smiled for the first time since they'd met at the Philharmonie's main entrance. It was hard to imagine that this exhausted-looking woman had only a year ago been a sprightly bundle of energy whose high spirits were almost unquenchable. Having once possessed all that mattered in life, she found that, with her husband gone, she had suddenly lost what rendered it secure and worth living. She now shared the lot of all women who had been unexpectedly exiled from happiness. Until the day when Jürgen deserted her, the status quo she'd attained had seemed to her to be the only worthwhile way of life. Was that why she'd thought it would last forever? No source of trouble, no one who wanted to share their happiness, no one who asked for anything she was unwilling to give.

Her luxuriant new hair seemed somehow to indicate that she was in search of a male substitute, and not only outwardly. She was on the old side but not yet old. She entertained hopes, that was the main thing; disappointment would follow soon enough. And miracles did sometimes happen.

So she started to talk about her new hairdresser, "the one who's recently been taken on by Salon Beige, you know the one I mean. I didn't know him at all and didn't really want to be served by him – 'served by', what an expression! – but how could I have told him so to his face? Or told Oliver, for that matter, who wished him on me? One doesn't do that, or at least, I don't and I didn't, either, and I really didn't regret it."

"I presume he's – "

At that moment Esther bumped into a short but not unathletic-looking man who looked up in astonishment from his cellphone – not an iPhone, she registered out of the corner of her eye – and promptly apologized, as she herself did. Was he astonished because of their collision, or because of the message he'd just read? Solveig gave her no opportunity to debate the question, she had the bit between her teeth.

"No, certainly not."

"Certainly not what?"

"I'm sure you thought he was gay, didn't you?"

"So he isn't?"

"No, absolutely not. The strange thing is, I thought he was gay just because he's good-looking and he behaves the way gay hairdressers behave – you know, nice and attentive and sharp-tongued and understanding toward women, when they aren't interested in you in the least, at most in your pubescent son – the usual thing, in other words. But I pretty soon realized I was wrong, he isn't gay at all, though not married either. So a kind of flirtation developed during the three hours it took to do the extension. We had a ball, in fact it might even be described as something else."

"And you really aren't wrong about him?"

"Why?" Solveig stopped short. She turned abruptly to Esther, who noticed at once that she'd committed a faux pas. "You mean if he isn't gay he was only nice because he pitied me?"

"No, of course not. Of course not."

She ought to have known that, since parting from Jürgen, Solveig tended to put the worst possible construction on any remark that lent itself to misinterpretation. Like now. Esther had to take care not blunder and exacerbate the misunderstanding still more. Solveig was in a fragile state even if she really believed the hairdresser had fallen for her, so she couldn't afford to ask if he'd called her or how old he was.

"Let's have something to drink, I'm thirsty," Solveig said abruptly. That made Esther prick up her ears. She'd been wrong. Either Solveig hadn't taken her unguarded remark the wrong way, or it hadn't sunk in. All the better. They went inside and made for the bar.

"And how is Thomas?"

"Sitting at home getting bored without me," Esther replied, trying to sound neither proud nor conceited, just flippant or ironical. It mustn't look as if she prided herself that her marriage was still working in spite of the children for whom she'd given up a lot that Solveig hadn't been prepared to renounce. Solveig had steadfastly and very successfully continued to pursue her profession until she eventually headed the legal department of the big private hospital in which she had started work as a young lawyer even before she met her husband-to-be. The culmination of her dual success was that he'd packed his bags and left her.

"No, seriously, he's very busy. He has far too much on his plate now that he's deputy medical director at the hospital." It was the hospital at which Jürgen, too, had worked before becoming self-employed. She hadn't gone to the lengths of not mentioning the hospital just because Jürgen had also worked there in the days when he and Solveig were happy together. It must have given Solveig a pang, but how could she have avoided it?

At the bar they ordered two glasses of Sauvignon blanc, and while Esther was taking her first sip, and even before she could say that the unmistakable, peppery aroma reminded her of the vineyards at Stellenbosch, she was astonished to note that Solveig was not only unabashedly surveying all the lone or unattached males standing around, but, once she made eye contact, staring at them in a brazen way of which Esther would never have thought her capable. At that moment, she seemed a totally different person.

Esther naturally refrained from commenting. Instead, she said, "You get a wonderful peachy aroma, don't you think? That slightly peppery aroma always reminds me of Stellenbosch. I don't know, though. This may even be a German wine." Did Solveig realize how oddly she was behaving?

"Yes, probably something from the Unstrut area," Solveig said with a shrug.

"They don't produce any Sauvignon," said Esther.

"No, but are you sure it's a Sauvignon?"

"Pretty sure. It certainly isn't a Riesling or a Müller-Thurgau. We did ask for a Sauvignon." She had no wish to continue this absurd conversation, but it was the only way of distracting Solveig from the lonely hearts she clearly wasn't embarrassed to ogle. She was highly relieved, therefore, when the gong sounded the warning to go in.

Klara and Sophie

"But I'd like a hot chocolate."

There wasn't any chocolate, either hot or cold, but Klara persisted as if her entire happiness depended on it. "I'm sorry." The girl behind the bar counter smiled and waited. She was very little older than Klara. She waited until Klara turned around, looking sulky, and simply left her aunt standing there. Sophie ordered a coffee and apologized.

"It doesn't matter," said the girl behind the bar. "It does," Sophie replied, and slid twice the requisite money across the counter. Why did she bother about Klara? "And please give me a large cognac." She put another disproportionately large sum on the counter without taking the change.

The more irrational and petulant Klara's behavior, the more strongly she reminded Sophie of her sister. Although she didn't resemble Alma in appearance, she was very much a kindred spirit. There was barely any difference between them. Klara had grown up, but it clearly hadn't improved her. Now that her protective childish innocence had evaporated, what had come to light no longer escaped Sophie's unerring gaze.

Sophie regretted having invited her ill-mannered niece and godchild to the Philharmonie. She also suddenly regretted paying eighty euros for Klara's ticket. It wasn't giving either of them any pleasure. Each was as patently uncomfortable as the other, the only difference being that Klara displayed her aversion openly whereas Sophie suppressed it. Self-control had never been her sister's forte; she should have known that her daughter would be no different. How strange that she had hitherto failed to notice that Klara was a carbon copy of her sister. She felt something akin to dislike for her.

"You might have been a bit nicer to that barmaid. How could she help it if your every wish isn't instantly fulfilled?" Her sarcastic tone hit the mark. Instead of being offensive, Klara looked offended.

"You're very like your mother. She was just the same at your age," Sophie went on. Her tone implied that she was acquainting her niece with a particularly unpleasant revelation, but Klara looked away as if she wasn't listening. Perhaps she wasn't interpreting Sophie's gibes the way they were intended. Nevertheless, she walked off.

Sophie drank her coffee and cognac at the bar, but she covertly watched her niece standing forlornly – or just with boundless nonchalance – among the other concertgoers. After draining her cognac in two gulps she felt strong enough to go over to Klara, for whom, now that the cognac had calmed her somewhat, she almost felt sorry.

"This concert isn't going kill you, you know. You'll live," she said when she reached the girl's side, but the joke fell flat although she had tried not to sound sour.

"Have you been drinking?" Klara asked abruptly, looking at her. Had she brought up some more guns behind her back?

"Why do you ask?" said Sophie.

"I can smell it."

So she'd opened fire.

"Let me worry about that."

"You've a problem with it, haven't you?"

"What do you mean, a problem?"

"You ordered a large cognac. Do you think that's normal? Now, I mean, just before the concert? A large cognac means you won't be able to drive, even after two hours. Don't worry, though, I won't wet myself. I'm not afraid of you or your driving skills. Not of you or my mother or Klaus. I can always take a streetcar home."

Klaus was Klara's new father. Klaus was her stepfather. Sophie was incapable of thinking clearly. After what she'd just heard, she was incapable of marshaling her thoughts. What had Klara just said? What? What was it? Had she been dreaming? Had she merely been fantasizing? She tried to believe she'd been dreaming. Where am I, she thought. At the Philharmonie. Exactly, that's where I am. That's where. Just before the concert. She felt as if Klara had slapped her full in the face. What to do? It was smarting. Hit back! Of course, what else! Hit back. She raised her hand, meaning to draw it back and strike, but missed the target because the target had already moved away. The target was a few steps further on. It had simply left her standing – standing in the midst of people, strangers. What did Klara think she was? Not an alcoholic, surely? She wanted to have it out with her – she had to clear this up right away. What did you mean? You think I'm an alcoholic, or what?

"Hello, Sophie, you here?"

She didn't recognize Solveig Schwarz immediately, her vision was blurred.

"Everything okay?"

"Yes, yes, I'm looking for my niece." She looked around.

Solveig, her colleague from the legal department – her boss, to be more precise, the highflier who had lost her husband on the steep ascent – was standing facing her. She was accompanied by another woman who gave Sophie a gentle smile as she extended her hand. They couldn't be serious! Why this effort to be cordial, this wearisome friendliness she couldn't reciprocate?

"May I introduce my friend Esther?"

Could they smell the cognac? Sophie barely opened her lips. Had the Schwarz woman turned lesbian since her husband ran off?

"Where on earth is my niece? I'm here with my niece. One moment. Klara?"

She simply left the two women standing there as if the said niece were a runaway infant that would get scared on its own in the crowd and start crying. Scared and tearful, that was how Sophie herself felt. What was she thinking of, that nasty, spiteful replica of her nasty, spiteful sister? Then, catching sighting of her already on the stairs, she turned and gave Solveig an apologetic wave, shrugged her shoulders, and walked off. Walked toward her godchild, taking care not to stumble or weep. She'd made a fool of herself. She would quickly freshen up first in the ladies'.

"Go ahead if you want," she said, half turning on her heel and handing Klara her ticket. "Ask one of the ushers where your seat is if you can't find it, I'll be with you in a minute." She felt she was making a calm and collected impression.

Courage! Freshen yourself up! Pull yourself together! She knew what irritated her about Klara. It wasn't the memory of Alma as a girl, nor the maddening impudence she displayed so belligerently, nor her indifference and other age-related quirks; it was the way she showed that she saw through her, Sophie. That was to do with Klaus. Klara sensed Sophie's envy – sensed that all that made her unhappy was associated with Klaus, Alma's husband, Klara's stepfather, and that she sometimes needed a bit of a drink to set her up and relax her. Without a drink she might have stopped venturing out into society altogether.

"Just going to freshen up," she muttered, but Klara couldn't have heard.

Esther and Solveig

"What's the matter with your colleague?" Esther was asking her friend Solveig at that moment.

"No idea. She isn't an easy person. We suspect she drinks more than is good for her – well, more than is good for any woman. Too much, in fact."

"At work as well?"

"At work especially, or no one would have noticed."

"Does that mean her job's in the balance?"

"We may suggest she seeks treatment before we chuck her out – if we feel we're compelled to."

"Are you responsible for things like that?"

"Heavens, no, that's the job of the director of Human Resources. I don't have to take care of it, thank God."

Marina and Johannes

He knew at once that he'd made the right decision when he called Accompagnato Berlin rather than any other escort service. The organizers on duty had obviously done their best to satisfy him yet again. Not because he was known to them, but because they endeavored to satisfy every client. One look was enough. It was a challenge. He recognized her at once – he would have recognized her among hundreds. That had to be Marina. What an unsuitable name for such a top-of-the-range creature. Top-of-the-range was the word for it. There was absolutely nothing repugnant about her. If there was anything that alarmed him, it was the fact that one couldn't tell how she earned her money, yet he had recognized her all the same. That was testimony to his knowledge of human nature. She was just what he'd wanted. It was as if she knew his most secret desires better than he did himself, because he wouldn't have dared even to dream of such a woman. She was simply stunning.

He felt convinced, even before she glanced at him, that the young woman sitting up straight on one of the white sofas and surveying her surroundings with apparent timidity must be the Marina whose name assuredly wasn't Marina but Meike, Mandy, or Steffi. The girl who would keep him company this evening.

Incomparable, his two-legged, one-purpose escort for the night, heaven-sent but terrestrially affordable. Just right for an angelophile like him. A shower of tinsel and a hint of plumpness about her face despite the high cheekbones, but nothing about this angel made an artificial, factitious, contrived, false, or bogus impression. She couldn't fail to realize how provocative and alluring she looked, and how well suited to her surroundings. Just a soupçon of naughtiness – no, less than a soupçon – but only a connoisseur spotted that sort of thing.

He grinned from ear to ear – he himself felt that no other description would have been more apt – and rejoiced like a little boy who has just hit the target with his slingshot. The window pane shattered with a loud crash, revealing the smooth, magnificent breasts of the woman who lived next door to his boyhood home, resplendent in all their alabaster glory behind the splintered glass still lodged in the frame. The sunlight impinging on the glass threw out glowing sparks that flitted to and fro and danced up and down on that agitated, milk-white bosom. Then the hand belonging to the bosom appeared. The damaged window swung open, scattering the luminous reflexes, which vanished, and her voice, instead of bawling him out, called, "Johannes! Come here! Come upstairs to me!" That was just the sort of bosom that was rising and falling beneath Marina's dress. She had made herself look very smart, neat as a new pin. The bird had fallen straight out of the sky and into his open arms.

She was quite tall, had long legs, and wore pale blue and white, colors that went perfectly with her blue eyes. Lying beside her was a big, pale brown, open handbag, probably Hermès. It was obviously expensive and of that unsurpassable lack of ostentation that testifies to the finest quality. The color of the bag contrasted only insignificantly with the color of her dress.

The young woman – she was no longer a girl – looked expensive and unaffected. She was worth the 180 euros an hour of which she probably had to relinquish half. Why hadn't she found herself a rich husband? Wasn't she looking for one, was she avoiding one? Was she frightened of excessive proximity and dependence?

The recognition signal was a gold, unopened cigarette case held in her left hand. A symbol of what it concealed? Smoking was naturally prohibited here as elsewhere. The girl on the phone had said, "You'll recognize Marina by a gold cigarette case. She'll be holding it in her hand, clearly visible." He thought he'd recognized her before that.

"Marina?"

She slowly looked up at him. No, she raised her head and opened her eyes at the same time. She had probably spotted him before he looked around for her in the lobby.

"Would you like to sit down, or shall we go right away?" Marina asked. He glanced at his watch and sat down. "I've a feeling we've met before."

"I don't think so," she said, but he had the vague feeling she felt the same. That was impossible, of course. They'd never met before, he would have been bound to remember.

"A pity one can't smoke in here."

She pointed to the doors. "One can smoke outside under the awning, it's quite mild today. May I ask you something?"

"Of course," he said, but it was a moment before she asked him if he was married. He nodded.

"Children?"

He nodded again. "Grown-up children. Great, big, healthy children, two boys and a girl. Plenty, eh? A wonderful, healthy, emotional little cross section of society." He laughed and she laughed with him.

"That's good. Yes, it's healthy. Let's go and smoke outside," Marina suggested. "It's not as healthy, but it's wonderful too."

No one had ever asked him such questions. They were on their own, no one else was sitting under the awning outside the hotel. They sat down facing the street with their backs to the windows. On their left the evening traffic was oozing down Friedrichstrasse.

"Don't worry, I won't bother you with any more questions like that," she said when they had sat down. She held out her cigarette and Johannes lit it. They smoked.

"All I like to know is that the gentlemen" – she said gentlemen – "I go out with don't have a bad conscience when I escort them or" – a little smile – "they escort me. It happens," she added because he looked at her inquiringly.

"What happens? Be more specific."

"Well, it happens that I'm asked to show the gentlemen around. They're strangers in Berlin, they want me to show them places they don't know. Mostly, though, I do exactly what's asked of me. In other words, I follow instructions." The implications of this statement didn't escape him.

"How about you?"

"Me?"

"Are you married?"

She shook her head.

"Children?"

She shook her head again and her smile froze for a moment. "Of course not." It was a second or two before she relaxed once more.

"I guess it's better if we skip the questions."

"It may not be better, but it's certainly nicer," she said. "I prefer a certain" – she almost seemed to writhe as she groped for the word – "anonymity. Sounds a bit banal, I know, but who isn't banal?"

"You aren't."

"Really? You think?" she said almost derisively, as if she'd often heard it before, and made a fleeting gesture that parted the cigarette smoke between them. She moistened her index finger, removed an invisible crumb of tobacco from her lower lip, and flicked it away. Was she aware of the erotic message of this series of mini-movements? It would have disappointed him if not, but he would never know.

There followed the usual phrases: "I love music. I love the Philharmonie. I love good food. I don't drink much wine – none at all, really, just enough to clink glasses."

It didn't really matter who uttered those sentences, they were interchangeable. And later: "I like traveling, I'd like to get to know the whole world."

"What's stopping you, Marina? Not that Marina's your name." He had uttered her name for the first time. She ignored the remark and he didn't revert to it, not wanting to be a killjoy.

"I don't know, maybe my lack of imagination." Maybe the lack of a man at her side? He wouldn't ask her. Other men were better left unmentioned tonight.

Another ten minutes and they had to leave. Johannes beckoned a waiter through the window and asked him to call a taxi, which pulled up outside the hotel three minutes later. When they were sitting side by side in the back, Johannes took Marina's hand and placed it on his left knee. The hand in his half-closed fist was almost weightless, little more than bone encased in cool, almost cold skin. How much did a woman's hand weigh, he wondered as he told her how tonight's concert-going had come about and that he was less of a music lover than she might think. It gratified him to note that she was impressed by his assignment in New York. Or was she only pretending to be? Wasn't that part of her job too? He might be wrong, she might be putting on an act, but he didn't care. He told her about the neurotic models because he felt sure she was quite unlike them – although she was slim, she had curves where they were macabrely bony – but it was clear that his description of them failed to impress her much.

It wasn't until she showed him the advertisement she'd torn out of the newspaper that he learned it wasn't a concert by the Berlin Philharmonic. The program featured no Mahler or Bruckner, no orchestral masterpieces but a piano recital by someone whose name meant nothing to him. "Should I have heard of him? Piano – oh God, if there's anything I can't stand it's piano music. It's pretty high up on my list of cultural dislikes, right alongside Proust and ballet. Shit – pardon me. Have you read any Proust?"

Meantime, he had been kneading her hand. He didn't want to disappoint her, but he didn't want to lie either. Not at the price of a lost evening that might first bore and then exasperate him.

"No."

"All the better."

"I'm not too sold on piano music myself," she said. She was telling the truth although it sounded like she merely wanted to oblige him. It wasn't far from that candid statement to her suggestion that they could simply forgo the concert altogether. "You need to have a good time, not torture yourself," she said. Yes, of course, Marina was right. Marina, what a silly name. It didn't suit her.

"Pity about the tickets, but what the hell," he said, and mentioned the name of a restaurant she'd never heard of, from which she inferred that he knew his way around Berlin. She hadn't expected him to make up his mind so quickly. His aversion to piano music was obviously extreme. "Do you know the Coeur Volage?"

She said no.

Two seats in the Philharmonie would remain empty; two tickets for which good money would have been paid by people who had failed to obtain any because the recital had been sold out for weeks. Others, who could not afford them, would have been grateful to be made a gift of them instead of letting them go to waste.

Johannes told the cabby their new destination and slid Marina's hand up his thigh. She naturally didn't recoil. It had already struck her that the man had no inhibitions, so there was nothing to fear.

"Let's have ourselves a special evening," said Johannes. To underline her acquiescence, Marina increased the pressure of her hand on his crotch and he gave a little groan, as she'd expected. But not loudly enough for the cabby, whose thoughts were probably elsewhere, to have noticed.

Astrid

Astrid looked at her wristwatch, then at the window. A few seconds before six. It was time to get up. Although drawn, the curtains were admitting enough light to dazzle her, or what she could still feel of herself. She had taken an Allegro and lain down as soon as she got back to the hotel. She was now feeling better, but she knew she was far from out of the woods. However remote the dull, menacing blows on the back of her skull might seem, they were not to be ignored. They could never be allayed. How well she knew this. It was nothing new. She mustn't think of it, must get to work, must get up and do what had to be done, must worry about Olsberg and not about herself. And refrain from thinking, either, that she was trying to do what years of experience told her was impossible: outsmart her migraine. She suffered from it just as her mother had done and recently also her sister, who was younger than her. In her mother's case it had calmed down and eventually fallen asleep altogether when she turned fifty-five, like a wild beast tamed by the loss of its teeth.

The concert was scheduled to begin at eight. In her experience, Olsberg would not start playing until five minutes past. Today as on other occasions he would give his listeners sufficient time to become sensitive to the moment when the first chord rang out. So sensitive that, depending on how he played it, they would feel it like a caress, a nudge, or a blow. For the ensuing two hours he would be in possession of what was once called their souls. He would capture and dominate them.

Astrid remained lying there for little more than a minute. Then she gingerly rose and crossed the room, one of the Adlon's smaller rooms but still spacious enough to make one almost forget that it was only a hotel room, not the suite Olsberg was occupying, on this occasion without a piano. He'd said he wouldn't need one after the long flight and in view of the fact that he'd just performed the same program in Tokyo. She opened the closet in which her clothes had been hanging since the day before yesterday and removed from its hanger one of the three suits she'd bought in Milan at the beginning of the year. She had developed the habit of indulging in this harmless annual extravagance years ago, just after Olsberg first employed her. She bought three suits a year. She hadn't so far worn out any of them. All were like new and all would probably remain so until the end of their life because she was extremely careful with her things. Olsberg himself had a soft spot for smart suits, expensive shirts, opulent materials, and tasteful accessories – Astrid knew the makes he favored. He was one of the few people, if not the only one, who noticed this luxury to which she treated herself, and which seemed so at odds with other aspects of her character. Noticing meant that he sometimes stared at her as if she were someone whom he didn't know, whom he clearly underestimated, and who could teach him things of which he had no inkling.

Astrid and Olsberg

Twenty minutes later Astrid and Olsberg were picked up, as arranged, by Verena Bentz's chauffeur. The Rolls was waiting outside the hotel surrounded by a bunch of curious, admiring spectators. It wasn't apparent whether the rubbernecks were attracted by the big, black automobile with the winged figurehead – the Spirit of Ecstasy, which the Germans had for some obscure reason christened Emily – or by the man in uniform, or by both. They included a few Japanese who had come from Pariser Platz and walked through the Brandenburg Gate. They clicked away without knowing whom they were photographing.

Olsberg, who had clearly been about to take Astrid's arm on the way to the waiting car – no, she wasn't imagining that because it wasn't unusual – looked as inscrutable as if his expression had the effect of a cloak of invisibility. She knew it of old. It was his way of cutting himself off. Whereas other pianists maintained a stubborn or diva-like insistence on sitting at the piano until shortly before the public were admitted, thereby causing the organizers extreme anxiety, Olsberg at this moment seemed interested in nothing but what no one save him could see: his own thoughts or those of them concerned with the immediate future. He had once told Astrid that he spent these pre-recital hours turning over in his mind's eye pages he often hadn't touched or looked at for years, indeed, decades. What was written on them was stored in that part of his brain that was most alien and mysterious to her, but in which he found his way around – she presumed – with the greatest of ease. However, what distracted people from him now was not his self-absorbed expression but the car they were getting into. No one seemed to recognize him, not even one of the Japanese girls, although he was a big star in Japan in particular, and not only since he'd lent his face and the ten slender fingers of his shapely hands to a world-famous Swiss watchmaker for advertising purposes and an astronomical fee. The late Mr. Hayek had doubtless been less interested in Olsberg's piano-playing than in the sound of his name.

It was unlikely that Olsberg appreciated or even noticed the fact that he was being driven to the concert in a Rolls. He leaned back against the cream leather upholstery and closed his eyes.

The curious onlookers gradually disappeared from Astrid's field of view as the chauffeur drove off.

The Rolls glided slowly and surely along as if it wasn't in contact with the ground. The driver became an ornament, his white-gloved hands seeming to hover above the steering wheel. They drove down Wilhelmstrasse, turned right into Leipziger Strasse, crossed Potsdamer Platz, and got to Scharounstrasse. Just before they passed the barrier of the artists' parking lot, Astrid noticed a cardboard notice being held aloft outside the main entrance by a fan who hadn't abandoned hopes of acquiring a ticket at the last minute. It read, "Olsberg Recital! Ticket Wanted!" If he was lucky he would be accosted in the next few minutes by someone unable to make the concert but loath to let their ticket go to waste. If he was unlucky he would retire empty-handed and spend the night in a bar or in front of the television with an Olsberg CD, but not at the Philharmonie. Disconsolate would then be the right word to describe him, or also, perhaps, furious and somehow offended at being shut out. Astrid wished him luck and smiled. It was the same picture in every city where Olsberg performed; the same excitement prevailed before his long-awaited appearance. Other people were also bound to be in search of tickets. Astrid reflected how lucky she was to be able to hear Olsberg whenever she wanted and wherever he was playing.

A few seconds later she was overcome by the wolf. It caught her unawares as usual, and as usual it was even bigger, stronger, and more savage than the last time: ravening, ungovernable, blind with rage. The pain was furnace red like its eyes and corrosive like its breath. Everything went black; the wolf had bitten her head off.

She only gradually attained the certainty that she was still alive. She was still alive, perhaps only so as to feel the pain. The wolf had crouched down. It was only a matter of time before it bared its teeth again, and more savagely. She belonged to it.

The next thing her gaze fell on was the big garment bag containing Olsberg's suit, shirt, and shoes. It was one of her jobs to look after this bag. What sort of state were the contents in! She spread her fingers and started to smooth the bag. God alone knew what it looked like inside. The suit, the shirt. She wasn't worried about the shoes, which she couldn't feel. The leather was fine and elastic. Shoes that pinched were unsuitable for concerts. When Olsberg put his hand on hers she said softly, "Oh God, your suit, the shirt, I'm sorry, I'm – an iron, my head, my head, I shouldn't have come, I'm just being a nuisance."

Olsberg got the picture. "Don't worry, Astrid. A few seconds won't make any creases, they'll be gone in a few seconds."

She noticed how quickly he withdrew from her. He had no wish to talk, not now. She could count herself lucky to have such an employer. He had other, more important things to do than cope with her annoying migraine and trifles like his garment bag. He needed to be alone and undisturbed, carefree and unimpeded. Who was she to distract him at such a moment? If only she'd already been there and he could have retired to his dressing room!

Explanations were unnecessary. Olsberg knew what the trouble was, even though she had never tried to make it clear to him – or anyone else – exactly what happened when the migraine assailed her, she wouldn't have found the right words in any case. But this didn't alter the fact that she felt guilty. It was stupid to hold her body or head or self responsible for things over which she had no control, but what in heaven's name was she good for tonight? The wolf lurking inside her skull might open its jaws again at any moment, and she knew it would do so sooner or later. Whether in one hour's time or ten, it would make its presence felt. She took care not to tilt her head or make any injudicious movement.

Olsberg was quick off the mark. He had gotten out before her, anxious to dispose of what awaited him as quickly as possible: the welcome, the kind words and best wishes. He always avoided shaking hands before a concert. People were familiar with this from other instrumentalists, and most of them refrained from obtruding.

He helped Astrid out of the car while the chauffeur, who had taken off his cap and clamped it – peak downward – to his chest, held the door open. Curiously enough, this starchy formality achieved the opposite of what was intended and robbed the situation of its gravity for a few moments. Astrid's view of her surroundings was slightly blurred, which always alarmed her although she knew it to be a natural concomitant of the migraine. Everything that now seemed abnormal to her was simply a side effect of her disease.

She would have to forgo sitting in the auditorium. Since the migraine could not be simply suppressed, she needed peace and – at least as important – darkness. She should really have gone back to the hotel, but she couldn't do that to Olsberg, couldn't leave him alone. She was still needed even if her sole purpose was to keep people from coming too near him before the concert. It didn't matter whether or not she was capable of thought. She wanted to be there for him even if she was beyond taking anything in. She would swallow another tablet as soon as they were backstage.

The manager was waiting to welcome Olsberg and his secretary at the foot of the steps beside the porter's lodge. He introduced himself, but Astrid didn't catch his name. She knew his name but it had slipped her mind. She was glad he spoke in a subdued voice, not for her own sake but out of consideration for Olsberg. Olsberg's manner was polite but aloof. He somehow conveyed that he wanted to talk as little as possible, and the manager got the message. He went ahead of them up the winding staircase and conducted them past the deserted canteen to the soloists' dressing rooms. The few people they passed on the way seemed not to notice Olsberg and Astrid at all. Either they didn't know who Olsberg was, which was unlikely, or they were taking account of his forthcoming strong-man act, for an evening-long recital of the kind that lay ahead of Olsberg was nothing less than that.

Sir Simon and his wife were waiting for him when they entered the spacious soloist's dressing room at the end of a short passage with other soloists' dressing rooms – not in use tonight, of course – leading off it. The scent of the lilies on a small table in the corner made Astrid experience the same nausea as that which overcame her as soon as she entered a florist's, together with the fear that she might have to vomit at any moment. She kept as far as possible in the background. Olsberg and Sir Simon were old acquaintances.

Astrid would have given a lot to be on better form – a lot, but how much? A year, a month, a week of her life? Eyes half shut and pained by the ceiling lights, she could scarcely make out the woman standing beside Sir Simon. "Nice to meet you," she said, "I'm Magdalena." The celebrated mezzo-soprano was as pretty as she looked in the papers, but all that she and her husband, who had just burst out laughing, said to her and Olsberg evaporated in the light she could hardly endure and the scent of the flowers that almost anesthetized her. She had to hold the wolf at bay. She should have remained at the hotel.

"Aren't you feeling well?" asked Sir Simon's wife, filled with genuine, unfeigned solicitude, and when Olsberg explained that his secretary was suffering from a migraine, Sir Simon, too, looked fleetingly concerned, though she might only have been imagining it. Meanwhile, she strove to preserve her composure.

Fortunately, nobody inquired how the disease manifested itself because anyone who had ever had a headache could well imagine what it must be like to suffer from one that was more unbearable than those familiar to them. After a few minutes' friendly conversation, Sir Simon and his wife withdrew and quietly closed the door behind them, having first satisfied themselves that this was what Olsberg wanted. "She's a great singer," said Olsberg, and Astrid nodded.

Then she, too, left him on his own.

The recital was due to start in an hour. Olsberg would devote that time to changing his clothes and effecting the transformation expected of him, the one he demanded of himself before every concert.

Astrid opened to door to the adjoining dressing room. There was a couch in there too. She swallowed the second Allegro and washed it down with some water from the bottle she always carried. She did not turn on the ceiling light but left the door slightly ajar so she would hear him if he called. When he left his dressing room she would get up and wish him all the best as she did before every performance. Then she would shut her eyes and hear and do nothing for the first part of the recital, just lie there moaning softly and allowing the pain's ebb and flow to wash over her.

Claudius

Claudius, too, applauded when Marek Olsberg appeared. He, too, stood up when – hardly had Marek set foot on the platform – some of the audience rose to their feet like cosmopolitan cognoscenti in New York, if only for the fifteen or twenty seconds during which he motionlessly maintained his bow from the waist. It was no pose, no affectation. When everyone resumed their seats they were back in Berlin. That, at least, was what Claudius felt.

The excitement Olsberg generated, even before he had played a single note, gave Claudius an opportunity to stifle the rage that pierced his breast like the red-hot knife of Mahler's traveling journeyman; to lay the keen blade aside, perhaps only temporarily, perhaps forever. The enthusiasm that greeted Marek was overwhelming. It overwhelmed Claudius too. Great though his chagrin was, it wasn't intense enough not to be drowned by the storm of applause, which Marek acknowledged with an indefinable, almost remote smile. How strange and incomparable a human habit, unknown in the animal world, was clapping, and how few were those privileged to enjoy being applauded. Discounting the annual singing of "Happy Birthday to You," applause was nearly always directed at others beyond most people's reach.

Having resolved to defy adversity and stay put, Claudius could find nothing better to do than merge as closely as possible with those around him. Their enthusiasm provided him and his mortification with at least outward protection and temporarily rendered him almost insensitive to his own misery. He stopped looking for Nico as soon as he'd sat down and nodded to a few familiar faces – yes, he was an esteemed, established, and even courted figure in the business, and this also consoled him for the humiliation he'd suffered and gave him fresh courage. Nico wouldn't come now, least of all if he kept watch for him; he was more likely to do so if totally unexpected. Claudius had in fact almost given up hope of seeing him again tonight, and he was preparing never to see him again in the future. So what? The less he hoped – thus his magic thought process – the more likely Nico would be to come back to him. There, he was thinking of him already! Desire and longing would overtake him and erode his superstition soon enough. His longing for Nico's skin – and all that went with it – could not be suppressed so quickly. But he would remain steadfast, he wouldn't make the first move, never! Not, at least, for the next few days. Not tomorrow, at any rate, and certainly not tonight. Secretly, however, he knew he was ready to crack. He wasn't a man of unshakable principles. Men with such principles were ludicrous figures; to be taken seriously, sure, but ludicrously normal. Not his type.

He was feeling sore and furious but didn't show it. That would have been out of keeping with his reputation and demeanor. It would only have harmed him. Someone who has been hurt doesn't mingle, he licks his wounds at home. He should do that all by himself, and if for once he does it in the presence of others, he should do it with due cynicism, loudly and clearly, in a discordantly sublimated fashion. Who apart from the person that couldn't see it would have delighted in knowing what was really going on inside him? Quite a few people, probably. He wouldn't even have begrudged Nico their malicious pleasure. For the sake of his love, of his attention – hell, of his youth! His twenty-four years, they were what counted! His white teeth, his sinfully shapely mouth, his silken skin, his firm flesh… He mustn't pursue that theme, for if he did he would instantly weaken and forgive everything.

Claudius was fiercely determined to enjoy the concert and look upon his former lover – Marek – as the good friend he had never become, even though that impossible normalcy had long been his dearest wish. Nothing remained of all his desires save the fact that he still represented Marek in Austria, Germany, and several other European countries. But not in the rest of Europe, not in North America or Japan.

Was he deluding himself, or had Marek really not aged since those days? He was now slowly turning to face the piano and making his unhurried way toward it. His movements radiated strength, yet they were totally devoid of tension. Unlike other pianists, whose movements on the platform were as stiff and awkward as those of marionettes, Olsberg made a self-assured, focused impression. It was inconceivable that anything could distract from what he now had to tackle. He moved with consummate grace, brilliant, dazzling, self-absorbed, self-confident. No, Marek hadn't changed. He was as attractive as ever. He seemed perfect, without a scratch, flawless.

And then he embarked on his rather unusual, unusually long program. It opened with two short sonatas by Domenico Scarlatti, a cheerful presto and an elegiac aria followed without a break by Samuel Barber's seldom-played and rather chunky Piano Sonata op. 26. In the program notes Marek had expressly requested that no one applaud between the two composers, so he wouldn't leave the platform. The overwhelming majority of the audience would accede to his request. Months ago, when he and Claudius had discussed the program on the phone, it had soon become clear that Marek would not budge an inch from it. Scarlatti, Barber, Beethoven, nothing else and in that order precisely. And after the interval some Schumann and two unspecified encores.

Claudius shut his eyes and, after the first few bars of Scarlatti's Sonata in A Minor, at once found himself where Marek wanted him and his other listeners to be: with him in a world in which sound consisted of himself and he of sound. The first part of the recital would, he had briefly estimated, last at least an hour – rather unusual for the pre-interval part of the program, especially as he would also be playing one of Beethoven's most demanding sonatas after the Barber, which was virtually unknown here.

Astrid

Astrid closed her eyes and almost immediately fell asleep. She heard nothing of what was going on around her. The wolf was still there, true, but it had rested its head on its paws and was now behaving almost like a docile animal. Did she really think that, or was she already dreaming it? Olsberg must have left his dressing room on tiptoe. He had shut her door, so it was silent inside, where she was resting. She did not hear the applause that rang out when Olsberg appeared on the platform, still less hear him playing.

Lorenz

orenz looked at the clock above the kitchen's double doors, which were wide open. Its dial was yellowish like the fingers of an inveterate smoker. An English model, undoubtedly, its dark case ringed with metal formed a pleasant contrast to the decor of the reception rooms, which was almost entirely designer modern. It was a few minutes after nine, possibly already time for the interval at the Philharmonie. Marek Olsberg, who would soon be a guest here, was a name that meant something even to Lorenz, who didn't care much for music aside from his inexplicable weakness for the North Indian tabla. Olsberg was well-known in the same way as the Eiffel Tower or the Empire State Building, which Lorenz also knew only from photos. A child prodigy, Olsberg had succeeded in preserving his talent into adulthood. That didn't go without saying, as no one knew better than Lorenz himself. It was just what he, who had once been regarded as a budding world chess champion, had failed to do. There came a day when he burned all the chessmen he owned in the garden. A purifying fire with no follow-up, redemption without liberation. He was a humble party waiter who liked sleeping late.

Standing at the stove, which loomed in the middle of the kitchen like a steamer with numerous masts and upperworks, were two fair-haired chefs resembling twins – pink-skinned, uncouth-looking fellows – and an Asian kitchen hand, a girl who could have been a boy or a boy who could have been a girl. Alongside those two overgrown babies the oriental creature looked like a forlorn, bewildered fawn.

They were arranging and decorating precooked food on platters that the so-called housekeeper had set out ready for them. Later, shortly before the guests arrived, they would freshly prepare whatever the catering center had already carved and partially seasoned: grilled and fried meats, precooked potato *gratins* and *crèmes brûlées* that had to go under the grill. The food Lorenz saw at these evening parties was not always the same, but for some reason people seldom departed from what was to be expected. There was plenty of money in this house, that was obvious. No expense was being spared.

Lorenz was not in the least interested in the various dishes' modes of preparation. Cooking left him cold, but he had to admit that the spread here smelled tempting. Certainly better than the two chefs, whose white shirts displayed sweat stains under the armpits and badly needed changing, at latest before Verena Bentz appeared with the first of her guests.

Although people were at work here, the kitchen was as quiet as an operating room – at least, Lorenz assumed that operating rooms were as quiet as this. He was used to different conditions. Unlike surgery, this work did not demand any special concentration; routine and experience were enough. He couldn't believe that a minor mistake would have unforeseen results. Perhaps the chefs were so taciturn merely because they'd had an argument. Perhaps they really were twins. Lorenz hadn't seen his sisters for some years. Their faces were just shadows to him. It was an effort for him to call them to mind.

"If you intend to be seen in public, and I guess you must do, you'll have to change. You can't go around like that."

He wasn't entitled to order them around, but it was fun. They couldn't assess his degree of authority because they were only employees themselves and did not come into contact with the public like him. At all events, his manner seemed to impress and intimidate them sufficiently.

"Okay," they said simultaneously. So they were twins or had developed into twins over the years, though they couldn't have had much time to do so, they were too young. The little Asian girl probably hadn't understood him. Her hands were enchantingly dainty and almost white. There was a glazed carrot sticking to her forefinger. She wiped her hands and – to Lorenz's regret – that jewel fell off into the trash can.

Shortly afterward they were joined by a man he had worked with on several previous occasions. Silvio, the Italian with a horde of children, uttered a loud and cordial hello and the atmosphere in the kitchen changed at once. Even the Asian girl smiled, even Lorenz's spirits rose, and all because of Silvio, the forty-eight-year-old paterfamilias who wore a thin gold chain around his neck and a thick one around his wrist clearly engraved with his name and not that of his wife Emilia, who, as he liked to proclaim with pride, still worked as a cleaner. It was all for the sake of the *bambini*, all *per l'avvenire*. She was the last Italian woman in Berlin to work as a cleaner. The others gadded around in the city center.

Employees of the catering company unknown to Lorenz had late that afternoon set and decorated the tables for the buffet on Verena Bentz's instructions. The floral decorations were superb: white hydrangeas and calla lilies in slender vases. Two rectangular tables had been pushed against the wall beneath the big picture windows while a circular one in the middle held the drinks that did not need chilling: red wines, various juices, and spirits. On each of the tables was a pair of solid silver, five-branched candelabra. The candles were not yet lighted. Lorenz looked at his watch. Twenty past nine.

Silvio had begun to talk about his family, his four children. Lorenz couldn't produce any stories of his own. They were standing in front of the cutlery cabinet, polishing the silver. Every knife, every fork and spoon was individually inspected, rubbed with a fine cloth, and held up to the light – a bright, friendly light that flooded down from the Venetian chandeliers suspended from the stucco ceiling. The plasterers had used pastel colors, and the molding had not been covered and coarsened by repeated coats of paint. This had preserved the delicacy of the original plasterwork, which had probably been applied a hundred and twenty years earlier by Bavarian or Italian master craftsmen. Applied was the right word for it.

Every detail stood out in relief, even the smallest flower, leaf, and stamen. Lime green, pale pink, Tieopolo blue – delightful. Lorenz tried to imagine spending his days in this place as the owner and occupant, not a paid employee. A seductive idea but not his destiny. He was and remained a party waiter.

Silvio, whose loquacity was beginning to weary him and whose recently welcome presence was now becoming a pain, was telling him about the progress and successes of his children in primary school, secondary school, and college. Lorenz felt convinced that the next time they met he would be confiding that his daughter Francesca had since married a lawyer or a politician and was five months pregnant, and that young Giglio or Gigi had won first prize in a science competition. He put Lorenz in mind of someone who spends an entire vacation in New York irritating other people by marveling at the fact that it's already eight in the morning at home when it's two in the morning there. He seemed unable to grasp the extent of his wondrous good fortune.

It was just after half past nine by the time they had checked the cutlery for traces of rinsing without finding the smallest blemish. At that moment the housekeeper entered the drawing room and announced that Verena Bentz had just called her. Apparently, she was beside herself.

Silvio and Lorenz stared at each other uncomprehendingly. Silvio didn't speak. That, at least, was a blessing.

Sophie and Klara

Who was playing, what was being played, what sort of instrument was it, was it a box? Coming from far away, the music surged and ebbed, faded, came and went, grew faint, ever fainter. Sophie lost her grip, slipped and slid off, sat up with a start, once, twice, slid off once more and drifted away. It was no use, her relationship to her surroundings had come adrift. Only half of her was sitting in her seat. The other half was escaping, and the part that had still been in the concert hall would follow. She had relaxed, had closed her eyes and admitted defeat. "Sleep is winning" – since when did she think in English? That she was asleep was not a deliberate act, not a decision or intention. Far from it, but sleep refused to be bamboozled or bought off, even by the great Olsberg, who was plying the keys down there, flailing his arms, pecking at the keyboard from above like a bird, leaning back, straightening up, crouching, stretching, merging with the black piano like a bat spreading its wings over its quarry, a whirring nocturnal insect in the innards of the instrument. For a few seconds she was awake, wide awake. The next moment she thought, Where am I? Was she awake or already in limbo? Was it a box?

During the third item, a strange piece, the Barber sonata she'd never heard before, she had at first been all ears, perhaps because it was new to her. At least for the first two movements. In the third movement – *Adagio mesto* – she had briefly nodded off, then sat up with a start when Klara's bony elbow dug her in the ribs. She very nearly uttered a startled cry. Had she been snoring? She didn't dare look around. How embarrassing.

After the furiously escalating fourth movement, a virtuosic, pounding, jazzy fugue whose wildly galloping leaps and audacious contortions she had followed with her senses alert, the concertgoers had risen from their seats en masse to vent their frenetic appreciation. She did so too, but Klara didn't. Klara didn't jump to her feet, just clapped a bit.

Olsberg was recalled to the platform five times, and Sophie had hoped that the commotion in the hall and the clapping would exert a lasting hold on her attention. She mustn't fall asleep at any price. She mustn't expose a weakness, especially as it would set Klara a bad example and give her another weapon capable of being used against her, possibly just for fun.

The first movement of the Hammerklavier Sonata blew her fatigue away, as it were, although the *Allegro*, as a surreptitious glance at her watch disclosed, was taking all of twelve minutes. Twelve long minutes during which she had no need to fight off her fatigue. This may also have been because of the heartburn to which she was particularly prone after drinking white wine, cognac or coffee, a condition that clearly occurred more often than was beneficial to her stomach. In short, she coped with the first movement – how many had he written? – brilliantly, without nodding off or dozing. But that was just the start. She dreaded to think of what was still to come: an endless multiplicity of notes and reprises, crotchets, quavers, semiquavers, demisemiquavers, minims, semibreves, triplets, dotted notes, pauses. She felt quite dizzy at the thought, felt weaker and weaker.

Then, after the second movement had flitted past almost unnoticed, came the third: *Adagio sostenuto*. Sophie's eyes suddenly snapped shut, and she'd been wide awake a moment ago! She wrenched her eyes open. A few seconds later the process recurred. Eyes shut, eyes open. Eyes shut.

For a while she managed to delude herself and anyone who might be watching her that she'd shut her eyes in order to concentrate on the music, as if that were the most appropriate way of absorbing the notes. Other people did this too, after all, and they quite often fell asleep, or fell asleep without making the slightest effort to prevent it. It wasn't long before this happened. She was exhausted by the whole thing. She was tired of the internal and external battles against opponents who mustn't be allowed to know that she was a victim and suffered from the fact – who didn't know this because her fate was a matter of supreme indifference to them. She was insignificant. Unimportant. Dismissed. She was uniquely uninteresting, in fact the word "uninteresting" seemed to have been coined especially to describe her. She was too old. She had been too pretty. This had stupidly given her ideas: the mistake made by all pretty women who fail to seize their opportunities by the scruff of the neck, even at the last moment. How long ago it all was. She had passed up all her opportunities. Back and forth, back and forth went her head, further and further downwards, not just sagging but dragged down, used by gravity as a guinea pig imprisoned in a diving bell and sinking ever deeper – now of all times, at a never-to-be-forgotten moment during a recital by Olsberg, whom many people justifiably compared to Horowitz although his touch was quite different. Who knows when you'll get another chance to hear him! All these things were going through her mind, through the convoluted white corridors and channels of her brain. She became lighter and lighter while Olsberg played and played and seemed to rock her in her sleep, send her from left to right and right to left like a weaver's shuttle in deft hands.

What was he playing on his black box? The question that arose before she finally fell asleep and her chin sank slowly on to her chest had some minutes ago prompted her to cast another glance at the programme, in which she could read what Olsberg had already played that evening and what he was going to play, but above all what he was playing at this moment, as she strove to decipher the print in the gloom. First the lively Scarlatti – the very name was programmatic – whose pieces had led her to attract looks from Klara, not that Klara had responded. There could be no talk of reciprocation; she had tried and her attempt had failed. She mustn't think of Alma, mustn't draw comparisons or commit injustices. No animosities, slights, insults, stupidities, hurts, resentments, hatred, contempt – she found it child's play to devise a thousand other words for the ten thousand emotions she experienced at the sight of the niece who was so like her sister. As revoltingly alike as a twin that had waited for years to hatch from its egg. A snake. Kill her if you dare, whispered a voice – her sister's voice – and Sophie wasn't surprised that Alma should urge her to murder her own daughter. Typical of her, she thought. Or had she thought that before? You wouldn't dare, whispered Alma.

It was all the same to Klara, of course. Why not, she had nothing to do with it aside from being Alma's daughter, and that she couldn't help. So Sophie had no choice but to be grateful because the girl had refrained from messing around with her cellphone, which would doubtless have caused a minor uproar in their immediate vicinity. Actually, Klara had turned it off before the recital began without Sophie having to ask her to. So she was behaving remarkably well, appropriately and *comme il faut*, even though the music visibly failed to interest her. Perhaps "visibly" wasn't the right word; it was more something Klara gave off, something that remained unsaid: I don't care, you carry on down there, okay, but leave me in peace, leave me out of it, I won't let it get to me. And she herself? Didn't the music bounce off her too like a wall, a lonely, looming stretch of wall like those that still stood here and there in this city, where she had lived for so long, as a forlorn-looking visual aid for tourists?

They were sitting in Block B, high up on the right. The auditorium was bathed in warm, luminous gloom. She mustn't fall asleep, because the music was bright and beautiful and she had a good view of Olsberg's face. What a privilege.

They were seated side by side like two close friends, but Sophie knew that Klara had long ago become her mother's reluctant proxy or doppelgänger, a clone, an avatar. She was doing the girl an injustice, of course, because she definitely wasn't to blame. But hadn't twice as much of an injustice been done to her, Sophie? The evil was deep-rooted in her sister's family. Why couldn't she change her spots? Why couldn't she concede that Alma had done her the worst turn anyone had ever done by luring her man away and stealing him within a few short days: Klaus, who had since become a sort of stepfather to Klara after her real father fled to the States from Alma's whims and demands. Perhaps she would tell Klara the truth about her mother and Klaus, thought Sophie, for she was almost sure that Klara didn't know a thing. How handsome and strong, vigorous and sensitive Klaus had been. The best man in her life, but what was that to the girl?

Had she thought all this while dreaming, while half asleep, half awake?

And then peace descended. She slept. She slept through the last movement of the Hammerklavier Sonata, the *Largo*, which was immediately succeeded by the *Allegro risoluto*. The fugue movement. The second fugue of the evening.

Silence. Absolute silence. Unexpected silence. Startling silence.

She would have to get Klara to tell her later what had happened, because she'd missed the unforgettable moment. What had happened?

Some three minutes before the end of the last movement of the Hammerklavier Sonata, that milestone in piano music, after around nine minutes' playing and shortly before he reached the end, Marek Olsberg abruptly stopped playing and slowly raised his hands. That the piece was unfinished and that he had prematurely cut it short – that something out of the ordinary was happening – at once became clear even to those who had never heard the sonata before and were not, or not yet, acquainted with the conventions of solo performances: Marek Olsberg shut the piano lid in a way that left no doubt as to the finality of his decision. And he said, in an expressionless but clearly audible voice, though not perhaps audible in every last corner of the huge building, "That's that."

As soon as Olsberg stood up and left the platform without a bow, without a word, utterly self-absorbed, indeed, detached from everyone, not hurriedly but not slowly either, all who knew him realized that he would not come back.

There weren't many of them, but they were supplemented by those who were more than usually sensitive to exceptional situations. Another few seconds went by, in the course of which Olsberg opened the side door himself and closed it behind him, and every last concertgoer in the Philharmonie became aware of the significance of what they had just witnessed. The ensuing commotion, which naturally remained within civilized bounds, began piano but soon swelled to a fortissimo. No mass panic, of course – the place wasn't on fire, after all, nor did everyone make at once for the doors, one or two of which had already been opened. Instead, people milled around, accompanying this spreading disorder with a vehement exchange of views. They were surprised, shocked, upset, appalled, infuriated, speechless, all in their own different ways.

Marina and Johannes

The features of which the Coeur Volage restaurant was particularly proud – according to its homepage – included its French head waiter, its "hand-cut baguettes", and the pleasant custom of welcoming patrons at the entrance before conducting them to their table. The harmonious interplay of the restaurant's sumptuously varnished wooden panelling, tinted walls, and numerous mirrors – to quote its own blurb – radiated a warm and cozy atmosphere. *L'esprit brasserie* was communicated by little details like the table layout and the pictures, but also the indispensable *carafe d'eau*, even if the carafes were filled with San Pellegrino instead of branch water. Only the elegant modern interior reminded patrons that they were in Berlin.

However, no one came to welcome them when they got out of their taxi and went inside. For a while they stood around at the bar on the right beyond the entrance and waited until an extremely pallid, pockmarked young man came up to them and inquired in fluent but French-accented German if they wished to eat. Yes, but first they wanted a drink at the bar.

"*Bien sûr*," said the waiter. Instantly, as if this was a prearranged codeword, another man materialized out of the background, who had hitherto remained obscure and somehow insignificant. This was evidently the bartender. He had a white napkin draped over his left arm and wore the same uniform as the waiter, but the contrast between them could not have been greater. He sported a positively repulsive tan and was hairy down to his fingertips. Johannes, who did not propose to enlist his talents, overcame his disgust of the man, who was waiting for him to order, and asked for a Pils. Marina ordered a glass of white wine. A Mosel, she said as if she knew the wine list – which she hadn't even glanced at – by heart. Did she know this place, or were Mosel wines now on tap in every bar in Berlin? Johannes had never in his life drunk a wine from there. It was the kind of landscape last familiar as a wine region to his grandfather, while grandma would at most have dipped a candy in schnapps. People moved in different spheres these days.

The bartender turned out to be French as well. He distinctly said, "Moselle, *bien sûr*," as he acknowledged the order with a benevolent, appreciative little nod. In his eyes she had clearly made the right choice. A dry Mosel. Johannes wondered if he'd missed out on a new trend. He would check Johnson's pocket guide and Parker's big one to see if there was anything he should know. The pockmarked man disappeared with their coats once they had intimated that they didn't want to see the menu until they were at their table. They sat at the bar, close enough for their knees to touch. Marina crossed her long legs, demurely provocative. She had put her handbag down on the nearest bar stool. The beer and the wine were simultaneously deposited in front of them with two sweeping, swooping arcs of the barman's hands. They raised their glasses and looked into each other's eyes. The atmosphere was faintly explosive, as it always should be in such circumstances. Characteristically, Johannes said briskly, "You can feel the electricity too, *n'est-ce pas*?" A smile flitted across Marina's face. "*Oui oui*," she said. Her "Vee vee" didn't sound as if she spoke the language, but perhaps she was merely pretending. He wouldn't have put anything past her, not even a university degree. She was mysterious and up for anything, that was what mattered.

"Are you from the area?" he asked her.

"From what area?"

"The Mosel Valley?"

She laughed.

"No. Why, do I sound like it? I honestly don't know exactly where the Mosel Valley is, apart from the fact that it's in Germany, of course."

"At least partly."

"What do you mean, partly?"

"Geography's obviously not your strong suit." She shook her head and he explained that the source of the Mosel, or Moselle, was in the Vosges – in France, he added in case she didn't know where the Vosges were.

He took her hand and kissed her fingertips.

"Not afraid of infection?"

He didn't let go of her hand as he shook his head.

He drained his beer in a few gulps and stifled the resultant belch. "I'm famished," he said.

"Me too," said Marina, so shortly afterward they were conducted into the restaurant itself, which comprised two rooms situated on different levels and connected by three steps. The wall mirrors barely disguised the fact that both rooms were only sparsely occupied. It was simply too early for Berlin. Most patrons did not appear until after ten.

Johannes decided on the table furthest from the entrance. He sat down on the faux leather banquette with his back to the wall, as if no one was to be allowed to see Marina from the front. All that anyone could see was her forehead in the mirror above his back cushion. He himself had a good view of both rooms from where he sat. He liked to be in control.

Marina could have been his daughter. It had to be that way, of course. If he'd preferred women his own age instead of young ones, Renate would probably have been enough for him. What pleased him less was the fact that he'd become aware of it at this moment. It wasn't that he was afraid of growing old or of being thought older – or younger – than his age. He might just as well have been afraid of the feminine sex per se because of their difference in gender. No, what worried him was the absurd thought of his daughter, of whom he had no wish to think and who worried him – his daughter, who naturally knew nothing of his escapades. What would she have thought of him, and possibly said to him, if they had come to her ears. Escapades! What an old-fashioned expression.

"I'm still a bit jetlagged," he said. "The older I get and the more often I travel, the worse it gets when I get back."

"I was in Asia once," said Marina.

"In Asia?"

"Thailand. I was surprised they don't use chopsticks there at all."

"Don't they?" He paused for thought. "Then I must have eaten in a Chinese restaurant there."

Again he got the feeling she was kidding him.

He often got the urge to eat a lot, sometimes immoderately and more than met with the approval of Renate, who noticed what his paid and unpaid mistresses saw but refrained from commenting on. They left remonstrances about his waistline to his wife, who, for all his itchy-footed way of life, got to see him more often than the other women he shared himself with. It didn't escape her that Johannes had been steadily putting on weight for several years and would have put on even more if he hadn't occasionally compelled himself to diet. On some of his numerous travels he picked up viruses that compelled him to spend hours on the john – an unpleasant thought he hoped would be dispelled by the order they were about to place. But they were still engrossed in studying the menu, which endeavored to emulate that of Brasserie Lipp or the Coupole. How successfully would soon become apparent.

Johannes decided on the classic steak tartare with *frites*, Marina on a small rump steak with *pommes allumettes*. He could only guess at whether she realized he would soon be tackling a plate of raw meat, but he felt pretty sure that, unlike other women who blenched at the very thought of uncooked food, she would be unconcerned.

"I wonder if he's playing already?"

He looked at the station clock that dominated the room and was modeled on the one in the Train Bleu – one of the handsomest and worst restaurants in Paris – before turning to Marina.

"He'll be doing his best whether he's playing or not," she said, "like all of us."

At that moment the waiter approached the table. He waited at a distance intended to leave no doubt of his inability to overhear their conversation.

"Would you like to order?"

They ordered.

"And wine! Lots of wine, please. More white from the Moselle, yes? No? All right, then bring us a nice Burgundy from" – he stressed the word – "Bourgogne."

The waiter gave a little bow and withdrew, looking rather disconcerted. Disconcerted about what?

"Ah, *autre chose encore*," Johannes called after the man, who promptly turned around. "*Quel millésime?*"

The waiter now looked thoroughly bewildered, not just disconcerted.

"I'm sorry?"

"*Le bourgogne que vous nous apportez est de quelle année?*"

The waiter came right up to the table. "Please speak German," he stammered.

"Why German? You're French, aren't you?"

"No. I'm sorry, I don't speak French. French isn't one of my – " he fell silent, then broke into an unmistakably Saxon accent.

"What?"

"We only pretend. We aren't French."

"What? You mean the guy at the bar isn't either?"

"No, not him nor the boss nor the chef. One of the kitchen hands speaks French, but he's from Ghana. Or is it Gabon? He's black, anyway."

"You mean you're fakes?"

"Well, we aren't French."

"But at work you pretend to be?"

"We have to."

"You really come from Leipzig, right?"

"Close. Dresden. Why, can you tell?"

"Sure can."

They both laughed heartily when the waiter – a touch more disconcerted than before – eventually walked off, looking like a con man caught in flagrante.

Esther and Solveig

"What now?"

Esther and Solveig had risen to their feet and were looking around uncertainly. Esther was clutching her purse. Solveig pulled her scarf too tight and promptly loosened it again. A subdued hubbub reigned.

The concertgoers couldn't express what they were thinking. They hadn't lost their composure despite being so abruptly jolted out of the state of mind that Olsberg had first created and then destroyed. What had happened? A few bars of music were missing, that was all, but what was wrong? Why had Olsberg denied them to his public? Esther and Solveig were certainly not the only people trying to grasp what had just occurred before their eyes and what a memorable occurrence they had just witnessed – a regular sensation which the media would be bound to make a meal of tomorrow and for the next few days.

"Do you think he blacked out?" asked Solveig.

Esther shrugged her shoulders. "No idea."

"Is he ill, do you think?"

"Yes, perhaps he's ill."

Esther couldn't produce more than an echo if she didn't want to start rooting around in the mists of her incomprehension.

The incident would trigger worldwide reports and speculation, for Olsberg enjoyed a worldwide reputation and what had just happened was certainly worth reporting. His premature discontinuation and abandonment of the Berlin Philharmonie's concert platform would cause a predictable, foreseeable furor. No arts section in any newspaper from the

Frankfurter Allgemeine to the *New York Times* would pass up the chance to report on it more or less extensively, glad of any opportunity to dish up sensations in a cultural field not exactly overloaded with them. After all, one couldn't always write about tenors shouted down because their vocal cords had failed, let alone about conductors who sexually harassed their male instrumentalists. The door had silently closed behind Olsberg, leaving 2387 concertgoers and several ushers nonplussed. The comments grew louder. Speculation could begin.

Silence. Tense expectation. No one had coughed as Olsberg covered the distance between piano stool and door. Everyone held their breath. Not a word had been uttered. What had prompted him to break off in the middle of playing, what was the reason? A disruptive noise that only he had heard, the Steinway, a sudden indisposition, a blackout, a gap in his memory? No one in the audience had ever experienced such a thing, yet nothing could really be more natural: a blackout, a gap in the memory, a sudden indisposition, an irresistible urge to urinate, a muscular spasm. Nobody knew except Olsberg. Perhaps he himself didn't know. Interviewers would press him to explain, intrusive questions would not be long in coming. The critics who were now leaving the concert hall without knowing how – or whether – the recital would continue almost unanimously reported that they had never before heard such a bold, modern, sublime, refined, noble interpretation of Beethoven's Hammerklavier Sonata as they had that night, and they doubted they would hear its like ever again. Or Olsberg ever again?

What had happened? What had triggered this incident? Why did such things never happen on other occasions? Those were only three of the many questions that hung in the air, unspoken and unanswerable. No one had held the stage door open for Olsberg, no one had shut it behind him. The platform attendant had missed his exit. No one had given him a signal, no applause had rung out that would have alerted him and made him jump up in time to open the door for the soloist, as he normally did. No unseen hand had closed the door behind Olsberg. He had done it himself of his own free will – a lonely decision. No one could explain what had just occurred. Olsberg had personally turned the handle of the door that led backstage, a gesture that illustrated how far he had thereby distanced himself from the tacit agreement regarding concert artists. This prescribed that they deigned to be human in public only to *seem* human, but were in fact semi-divine and thus could not spare a hand to open and close doors themselves. Their fingers were reserved for other, more important activities. Such were the thoughts that passed through the minds of the frustrated concertgoers who now prepared to leave the auditorium.

Once the initial commotion had subsided, they were overcome by an almost palpable feeling of dejection and disappointment. They closed ranks. Strangers conversed with strangers. Views were exchanged. Disenchantment, disappointment, disconcertion. Within a few seconds the Philharmonie was bathed in different lighting. The management had turned the lights up. By now, most of the intimidated concertgoers whom Olsberg had cheated out of the conclusion of his interpretation of the Hammerklavier Sonata had risen to their feet. They looked around in dismay. What to do, what had happened? Had he really said "That's that," or had they only imagined it? "That's that?" How incredibly out of order, or had they misheard? Questions, questions. They still seemed unable to decide whether to leave the auditorium for good, as if some other trouble spot was waiting to flare up. A few steadfast souls hoped that Olsberg would return, resume his seat, and complete the sonata – play the whole of the last movement from the beginning, but nothing happened. No organizer showed his face or explained the pianist's behavior. Nobody came out and apologized.

The question of what would happen now was only gradually succeeded by the realization that it was unlikely anything would happen at all. "That's that." Olsberg actually had said them, those out-of-order, out-of-character words; he'd said them and the people in the first few rows had distinctly heard them.

"Do you think he's ill?" asked Solveig.

"Could be."

"He'll come back, though, won't he?"

How could any of them know?

"No idea. We'd better wait out the interval and see what happens."

Shortly after the auditorium had emptied, barring a few elderly folk, several loudspeakers broadcast an announcement that the recital could not be resumed, but that consideration would be given to exchanging tonight's tickets – which kindly retain – at a later date. Further information would be obtainable from the box office by phone from ten a.m. tomorrow. The management greatly regretted the incident but wished everyone an enjoyable evening.

"Very nice of them. So what shall we do now?" asked Solveig. She got the impression that Esther was less unhappy about the unexpected turn the evening had taken than her, who still briefly hoped to be able to get something out of it. "What say we go and have a nice meal or a drink? It really isn't late."

Esther didn't think for very long before replying that she was tired and had something to discuss with Thomas. She promptly tried to reach him on her cell phone but failed, probably because he had fallen asleep in front of the television, as he so often did, or had already gone to bed.

"I'd sooner make it another night, when we've got more time. Besides, it's depressing somehow."

Esther sounded rather abstracted, as if she were itching to be off. She made for the cloakroom with Solveig in tow. She was wholly indifferent to the latter's ideas of how they could still bring this incomplete evening to a worthy conclusion. No wonder she made an inconsiderate and selfish impression on Solveig, who experienced a sudden feeling of belligerence – not for the first time, now she came to think of it.

Esther wanted to get back to Thomas as quickly as possible and bring about the state of affairs she had ardently but vainly desired before going out: she wanted to join him on the sofa, drink a glass of Chablis or Sauternes, eat a slice of foie gras, let a spoonful of Mont d'Or or Brie de Meaux dissolve on her tongue, take a couple bites of baguette, and zap from channel to channel while Thomas massaged her feet, kissed her ankles, her knees.

On the way to the cloakroom she turned to Solveig and said, "I'm on a diet, I can't eat anything more at this hour in any case. Please don't be hurt, but after this fiasco I don't feel like anything at all, you know? Not even a glass of wine."

She was lying and felt sure Solveig noticed. Solveig merely nodded without a word. Did the fact that she was lying so shamelessly mean she didn't regard Solveig as a friend, just as a useful companion?

Esther proved to be quicker, more nimble, and more determined than the other people who were making for the cloakroom and rather half-heartedly trying to get their coats back. She forged a path through them and soon reached her goal.

While Solveig was slipping her left arm into the sleeve of her coat she felt someone behind her trying to help her on with it. She guessed who it was before she turned around: Sophie something. A good thing people used first names in the firm. It was hard enough remembering those; remembering surnames as well would have been far too demanding. For Solveig, at least, though possibly not for other people. She regarded her inability as a mark of authority, not as a shortcoming occasioned by advancing years. She could afford it, other people couldn't. This woman, for example.

Graciously and, she hoped, with sufficient detachment, she said "Thanks" as if afraid that Sophie might take it into her head to want to spend the rest of the evening in her company. Of course she didn't. Certainly not. Someone like Sophie would never dream of such a thing. Her proximity was fortuitous, not deliberate. The Philharmonie was a big place, but not so big that your paths couldn't cross twice the same evening. How would this woman have known where she'd dumped her coat? Still, this considerate little gesture obliged her to take a closer look at Sophie's niece, who was standing a little to one side. An extremely pretty creature, she noticed – not without a pang. Was that how she should envisage her husband's mistress? Like her or similar? Yes, exactly like her, though a few years older. This girl here must still be in school. All the more attractive to a husband like hers. Why on earth did she feel so lonely?

"Thanks, I can manage." She looked around for Esther, whom she had suddenly lost sight of.

"See you tomorrow or sometime."

She spotted Esther waiting in silence near the exit with her cellphone clamped to her ear. It suddenly occurred to her how absurd it would have been to feel smug, had she been able to tell Esther she was going off for a drink with her colleague. She was loath to imagine what an impression that would have made on her friend – her friend, who was leaving her in the lurch.

Outside, people were waiting for non-existent taxis. News of the recital's premature conclusion had obviously not yet reached the various cab companies. This intensified the demand for the few cabs that had appeared during the interval to pick up those concertgoers who, experience told them, were forgoing the second half of the program. Solveig drew a deep breath. What a depressing evening! What a pointless waste of time!

II

Marek

He had never before felt so free. The space around and within him was light and airy. He was free.

It wasn't as light backstage, but light enough for him to almost effortlessly find the way out past a man sitting hunched on his chair. The man whose job it was to open the door for him, and who didn't know what to think because he couldn't immediately grasp what had happened. Who looked up in dismay. Who jumped to his feet but didn't know what to do. Marek felt the man's gaze on the back of his neck. He had opened the door that ultimately led to freedom by himself. He was leaving all that was familiar to him and entering a place where all was unfamiliar and no one knew him.

He was not following any plan. It had happened not against his will but fundamentally without his doing. That, at least, was his impression. When he appeared before the public tonight, his sole intention had been to play the program as printed. The way he had done for years, and the way he would doubtless have recorded it tomorrow in his current oilcloth-covered notebook had everything obeyed the usual rules on this occasion too. He had appeared before the public, who revered him like an immutable, immaculate genius complete with cornucopia, a man who had only to move his fingers to attract their attention. His private life was no more public than that of most classical musicians, whose personal lives – discounting a few operatic divas – aroused remarkably little interest. It was as if they paled as soon as they ceased to be in contact with their instruments, as if they didn't exist at all without them – as if they were vampires who lay motionless in their vaults, waiting until nightfall to lift their coffin lids and appear. He had entered the auditorium only to end by disappointing it, but he was free, and that was what mattered.

In a trice, Marek had changed the direction of his life, of his effect on the outside world. It was a radical change, and all the more radical for being unintended, in other words, a surprise to himself as well. The consequences would be correspondingly significant, but he had no wish to think about them until later, if at all. It was still too soon.

He had acted between two breaths, precipitately and out of the blue, but he had acted. Breathing out is more important than breathing in, Wilhelm Kempff had once told him in Positano. He had adhered to that principle when playing and ceasing to play. He had never before wasted any thought on this simple solution – the obvious solution. No, he had never even dreamed of it; he never dreamed of the hours he spent at the piano, whether at home or in public. He went through those hours as if asleep. His life had gone off the rails. He was alone. He was free. No one was following him. He must be rather like a suicide who pursues his objective regardless of what other people think and without looking back. He had gone off the rails so as to branch out in all directions.

He was familiar with the Philharmonie from previous appearances there, but far from familiar enough to find his way around the building easily. He did, however, recall that there was a rear exit accessible by way of a flight of stairs that led to the parking lot one or two floors below. No one would notice him if he was quick. So he hurried. Nobody was following him, the rooms backstage were deserted and in darkness. He wanted to get out of there. Resolutely, he made for the dressing rooms. He took his coat from the hook and looked around. He had all he needed. Astrid had evidently noticed nothing. She was lying asleep in the adjacent dressing room. The door was ajar. She had probably taken some strong medication for her migraine and turned out the light. She would see to his things. He was feeling young and chipper, released from the prison of other people's – strangers' – desires. Set free.

He found his way to the staircase and reached the first floor, more than once taking two stairs at a time. He was feeling as carefree as he had when he won the Grand Concours de Budapest, one of the youngest competitors and, in the end, the youngest winner. The world had been his oyster, and now it was so once more. Possessed by this feeling of deliverance, he emerged into the open. It hadn't occurred to anyone that he might decamp like this. The manager, who had been seated in the directors' box, was probably busy placating the agitated souls around him. Anyway, Marek hadn't bumped into him. The man was probably making for his dressing room right now. Too late, my lad. What would Claudius say? He hadn't so far given any thought to his former lover and longtime agent, and he didn't propose to do so now. He had long ago freed himself in that respect too. Would his exit have financial repercussions on Claudius? They certainly would on himself.

Anyone who thought he was in his dressing room and would return after the interval, as if nothing had happened, would be disappointed. It wouldn't be long before everyone realized he wasn't going to reappear tonight. Or any other night, probably. Perhaps this part of his life had ended tonight. There was no going back, just freedom. That was it. Grinning to himself, he walked across the parking lot unnoticed. Turning up his coat collar was enough to avoid recognition. He wouldn't wait for a taxi but set off on foot and go and drink a beer someplace. A beer! What a splendid idea. What fun.

Marek Olsberg had disappeared in the interval so as to go and drink a beer someplace! He couldn't hoist it in himself and had to restrain himself from behaving too conspicuously. Being recognized was the last thing he wanted. He felt like singing and dancing in the rain *à la* Gene Kelly, who had pranced and tap-danced through puddles until a cop caught sight of him and put an end to his clowning. He had said what had to be said. He had quit the dungeon he'd entered a long time ago. It had been a fine, luxurious dungeon of continental dimensions, but a dungeon all the same.

Marina and Johannes

She turned away, got to her feet, and went into the bathroom, where she quietly closed the door and gargled without looking in the mirror. She had left her handbag in there. It contained all she needed. This wasn't her first visit to the hotel. She knew it of old and would return. The bathroom wasn't very big, but there was room on the marble shelf for everything from shoe-cleaning sponge to shower cap, chromium-plated Kleenex box to bubble bath and shampoo. She didn't touch any of them. She glanced into the sponge bag of the man who may have believed that he'd just been very intimate with her.

The client was asleep. She had recognized Johannes Melzer at once – almost as soon as he opened the elevator door in the Westin Grand. A sachet of white powder was nestling against his identity card. She hadn't touched it. Melzer was one of a kind. Self-assured, well-educated, witty, dashing, good-looking, he was one big cliché of a man who confidently, if not arrogantly, marketed himself as "successful."

He had made it. They had both made it, her father in his way and Melzer in his. Neither of them could be allowed to know how Marina earned her living, neither Melzer nor her father had the least idea. What a scandal if her father had learned it from the lips that had just been sucking her nipples and kissing her lips and body. He would never do that to his best friend. It was easy to imagine how deeply such a revelation would have shocked and hurt him. The fact that she had run into Melzer wasn't fate but pure coincidence.

A coincidence that had to be taken into account. He was ignorant of that coincidence.

Johannes Melzer, college friend of her father's, friend of the family, fond of children, and locally important figure, had obtained an arts degree but taken a different route to her father, one that led to the world of advertising, a route that was up his street because it also had to do with words – words that charmed, enticed, and convinced. His daughter Susanne had been her best friend until she moved. It was a long time since she'd seen her too.

Actually, he would have made an ideal godfather. She didn't know why her parents had chosen someone else. She had never forgotten the omnipresent Melzer. The families had celebrated New Year's together, rented vacation homes together in the summer. It was no wonder Melzer hadn't been able to keep in touch with her, what she did now was too remote from the old days. Too remote from the cute little girl in white bootees.

He hadn't recognized her. She had simply reminded him of someone. Not of Bettina Sorge, but of someone unknown. She had been thirteen when Melzer and his family moved to Düsseldorf, the Mecca of the advertising trade, as it was called. How long would it be before it occurred to him who she reminded him of? Probably not while they were together. Later, perhaps, when the spatial and temporal distance between them was great enough. Perhaps never. At this moment she was far too close to him, her physical proximity hindered recognition. But when the distance between them was big enough – in the plane or the inter-city express going home, or when he saw her father again – the scales might fall from his eyes. What a shock! Or not?

She could have learned from him and her father what a help and a bond friendship is. She was thirty-one and had no friends. It was pretty certain she would still have no friends at forty. She felt for her handbag with her eyes shut. She didn't want to open them. She felt the soft leather against the back of her hand.

They were bound to be friends still, her father and Johannes Melzer – it was inconceivable that anything could ever alienate them, different though they were. That difference was the secret and basis of their friendship. Her father was a remote, cloud-wreathed figure with a capacity for unexpected flashes of brilliance, Johannes a man of action, a macho, a star, forever with his finger on the pulse, as wealthy as he was generous, with a wonderful, understanding wife at his side, more an equal partner than an accessory. If Marina had had a sister he would probably have recognized her had they resembled one another, she and her non-existent sister. Her brother bore no resemblance to her. He took after their mother, whereas Bettina might have been placed in the nest by some alien hand. She was too far removed from the mental picture Melzer might have of her, unless he'd simply forgotten the girl she used to be: Bettina, whom he'd once dandled on his lap. As a little girl she had felt closer to him than her stern, humorless father, whose jokes – if any – tended to be told at other people's expense. Then and now. What a difference!

What could she do with this information, the knowledge that it was really him? Nothing. She lacked the imagination for illegal acts. Blackmail, extortion? Torment him a bit? She lacked not only the imagination but also an incentive, a reason. She had no motive for punishing or scaring him. No, that would be simply absurd. She was feeling tired. She ran her fingertips over her face from forehead to chin, three or four times. Tonight would earn her a lot over and above the fixed charge. His pocketbook was stuffed with 200 euro bills, and there was also a 500 among them. If she knew him, he wouldn't be content to fob her off with the agreed fee.

He'd been lying on his back, naked and uncovered, when she left the bedroom. That was probably how she would find him when she returned. He was sure to have fallen asleep. She would cover him up as soon as she'd completed her toilette.

She sat down in the bathtub and briefly showered herself from the navel downward. It wasn't hard to insist on prophylaxis. After all, it didn't mean being standoffish. She had no difficult clients – difficult clients moved in different circles. Anyone who wanted to do more than touch her – in other words, anyone who had professional dealings with her – had to wear a condom and did so. There was nothing doing otherwise. Most of her clients were men of a certain age, but they weren't tired of life. On the contrary, the older the clients the more careful they were where potential risks were concerned. Very few of them had no experience of extramarital relationships, paid or unpaid. Anyone who didn't know the score could consult the Internet. How many deaths could have been avoided in the sixties if there had been search engines to warn of dangers that were then almost unknown. What did people die of today, for God's sake? Cancer and unrequited love, like the old days.

She dried herself. The towel was soft. The hems – the Achilles' heel of any hotel towel – displayed no noticeable signs of wear. They, too, were impeccable.

Marina got out on to the bath mat and looked in the mirror. She repainted what needed repainting, her lips; tinted what had lost its color or become smudged, her cheeks; and put up what had come down, the hair behind her ears. Was that her body? She nodded. Her face? She nodded. Little needed to be done to restore the façade. The windows were impenetrable even though the eyes were open. She saw enough, no matter what others saw. There had been so many 200 euro bills in his pocketbook he wouldn't have noticed if one were missing, but she naturally hadn't taken any of his money. Criminal acts cost you your job and she didn't want to lose it. It wasn't worth it, not for 200 euros. Stealing never paid.

The door opened and Melzer was standing there in front of her, looking stunned. She'd been wrong, he was gazing at her in horror. She hadn't expected this, felt as if she'd robbed him after all.

"For God's sake, you're Bettina. You are, aren't you?"

"Did you root around in my things? That's not nice."

"Don't be funny. No, of course not." He struggled for words, quite unlike himself.

"What are you doing here?"

"I took a shower."

"I mean, what are you doing *here*? What sort of – is this your job, is that it, eh?" For the first time she was confronting a man who had lost his composure, someone with incredulity written all over his face – stock phrases that had materialized into a moving image right before her eyes.

"Is this why you left home? What are you doing here?"

"I trust I performed my work to your satisfaction?"

"Don't be funny."

"I'm here to work, and after work I shower. My name is Marina, I don't know who you're talking about."

"I'm talking about you, Bettina!"

"Bettina was then. My name is Marina. What do you want of me?"

"Nothing." Then, much more softly, almost whispering, "Nothing."

They had gotten over the most dramatic moment. Unlike him though it was, but he perched on the wet rim of the bathtub and, almost as if asleep, as if he weren't on the ground but hovering in mid-air, began to speak in a monotone.

"I'd fallen asleep, then I woke up. And then I suddenly, almost instantly grasped the truth and knew who you reminded me of. Of Bettina, of course. She reminds me of my best friend's daughter, I thought, his Bettina. We missed her. At first we missed her, then we gradually forgot her, we did anyway, your parents didn't. And then, suddenly, the scales fell from my eyes. It really is you. Of course you're Bettina. What are you doing here? Why? We wondered for years what had become of to you. No one can't simply vanish off the face of the earth."

His voice, which had grown steadily quieter, died away altogether. Tentatively, almost shyly and with surprising diffidence, he stretched out his hand toward her face and raised it level with her forehead, but didn't touch her. He lowered his arm and looked at her inquiringly.

"Yes," she said, "you can if you want to." After a while she went on, "I don't want to talk about it. Talking about it is unimportant. The old days are all so remote. Just as remote as they should be. Nobody asks you why you do what you do. Why you didn't stay in your hotel room tonight or go to the concert on your own. Or why we didn't go to the concert together. I've never been to the Philharmonie. What did we miss there that we didn't miss here? This is fine. For you and me both. That's all. We aren't getting all moral, are we?"

"But what are you doing here?"

She gave a laugh, and it didn't at all sound bitter.

"The same as you, perhaps, except that I earn my living at it. I go to bed with strange men, that's all. And I'd like to travel a lot, but I don't. I'll go traveling more often when I've saved up enough."

She could positively see him pulling himself together and regaining his composure. He was almost the old Johannes Melzer when he straightened up. Not the kind of man to mourn the innocence she'd lost a long time ago.

"Ah well," he said before leaving the bathroom, "at least it wasn't incest, was it?"

"No, nor pedophilia." And, given that he was a good-looking man, what they had done together would not have been unacceptable even if she'd done it on a momentary whim instead of for money. There were plenty of whims a person could succumb to.

Esther

She had actually made it. She was sitting in a taxi she'd flagged down on Potsdamer Strasse. She sat behind as usual. It was a long time since Berlin cabbies had expected you to keep them company on the passenger seat. On the contrary, that often served as a repository for things that accumulated within their own four walls as well: odds and ends, knick-knacks, torn paper bags containing long-life foodstuffs, articles of clothing, cigarettes.

The cabby's cracked leather jacket and the green upholstery gave off a smell of stale tobacco smoke. It had started to rain. She shivered. The evening had turned cool. Summer was gradually giving way to fall, a first foretaste of a long winter. Warm days, cold nights. She should have dressed more warmly. She looked at her watch. It was nine-twenty. Thomas must have fallen asleep – she had called him twice from the Philharmonie and he hadn't answered. She would try him again in a minute, tell him about the concert's surprise ending and her premature return.

"Oh!" Her cry of astonishment made the cabby jump. She thought she had identified a man hurrying in the direction of the Sony Center as Olsberg. But that was impossible, of course. A man like him did not cross Berlin on foot. The figure vanished into the darkness like a phantom. What if it really had been him? Nothing seemed improbable to her tonight. It was improbability that was lending the evening its special quality. Perhaps she hadn't been mistaken. She sat back against the upholstery. She was secretly convinced it had been him, and for a moment she regretted not having told the cabby to pull up. Still, what business of hers was Olsberg except when performing in public? Didn't people say he was gay? She wanted nothing to do with gays; more precisely, she didn't know any. Her fear that Gustav might develop in the wrong direction had proved groundless. The fear of all mothers.

"Do you know much about gays?" she asked the cabby abruptly.

"I'm sorry?"

"Nothing. Just a thought." He probably hadn't caught what she'd said.

An evening with Olsberg, she thought. Who would have believed it?

"It was just a thought," she repeated, and laughed. He didn't laugh, eyeing her in the rearview mirror.

She called again to tell Thomas she'd be home in around fifteen minutes, but he didn't pick up. His voicemail voice cut in eventually, but she didn't leave a message. She'd be seeing him very soon. She guessed she would catch him asleep on the sofa.

Nico

Without bothering which movie it was, what it was called, and who had directed it, Nico bought a ticket for one of the nineteen multiplex screens – No. 7, which had already started showing the movie, seven being his favorite number – in hopes that the fast-changing images of unfamiliar places that would soon bombard his eyes and the unrealistically loud sound of punches landing and doors creaking that assailed his ears would take his mind off things and calm him down, because he was still upset. Claudius's renewed refusal to ease him into a better job more suited to his abilities was – of this he felt convinced – simply an expression of his low esteem. Of his disdain, not to use the more appalling word contempt. No, Claudius did not despise Nico, he was too handsome, too seductive and unspoiled. But not an equal partner, not on the same plane. At best, from another star which Claudius would never reach, but a star whose luminosity was imperceptibly fading with every day he grew older.

He didn't want to think, he wanted distraction. Hurriedly, he elbowed his way past the other moviegoers and promptly plunged into the unreality of a form of lighting obviously designed to give the audience the feeling that they were part of a movie whose course they could determine themselves – more of a cartoon than a feature film, anyway. It was just before half past eight, and the movie Nico didn't even know the name of had been running for half an hour. He would find it hard to grasp what it was about.

The auditorium was half empty. Nico sat down in a seat on the right-hand side and shut his eyes. What he heard were cellos trilling and dubbed voices that sounded familiar, so it wasn't a German movie. A car drove up, a door slammed shut, footsteps on gravel. He opened his eyes. He had seen the actor before. Not a star, so not the principal character. A young, fair-haired woman came up to him, kissed him, then turned away without a word. Nicole Kidman, he thought, but that was impossible, the movie was brand-new and there weren't any new movies starring Nicole Kidman. For several seconds the camera concentrated exclusively on the blonde beauty's pelvis. Nico looked around. The row behind him was as deserted as the row in which he was sitting. When he looked back at the screen the woman had a knife in her hand and was stabbing the man. The victim's blood spattered her face and spurted over her shoulder from the dying man's carotid. The concert at the Philharmonie had already started. He had passed up the opportunity to meet Olsberg. What would he have said to him, anyway?

As soon as he thought of what he was missing while staring uncomprehendingly at the huge screen, which was now bloodless again, rage blazed up inside him once more. Anger could not be quenched as quickly as it was ignited. Had he allowed Claudius and his emotions to get close to him only because he was what he was: an influential concert agent who earned a lot of money, socialized daily with interesting people, and would, Nico hoped, introduce him to them? And who was nearly thirty years older, which reduced the prospect of a longish relationship to a short-term episode. And who lusted after him no matter where he worked and what his school grades had been. In order to make a real impression on Claudius he would have had not only to look like a young Joshua Bell but be able to play the violin as well as Bell, with those soaring, half awkward, half imperious, somehow ecstatic movements Nico had admired, not without envy, on a TV recording. Wow, great, anyone who can play like that must have the world at his feet. And the world did indeed lie at Bell's feet as it did at those of Olsberg and all the other people Nico couldn't hold a candle to.

But he was shorter than Bell and didn't look like him. He might be prettier than Bell had ever been – that was a matter of taste – but he couldn't read music, far less play an instrument. He didn't have perfect pitch. The most he could lay claim to was a sense of rhythm, but that he didn't have to prove except when dancing. He would grow older, and unlike piano or violin virtuosi he would not mature in any respect save possibly in his desire to be able to do something not everyone could and, above all, something he could not. All that remained was his vague affinity with music, which – as he knew better than anyone – was far from enough when you wanted to hold your own with musicians. Even a simple conversation with a trained musician would floor him, he knew, and he didn't have much with which to offset his limitations. His good looks, but good looks did not have as potent an effect on everyone as they did on Claudius.

He knew that it was more than just a hunch when he kept recognizing similar and varying melodic sequences in the works of Richard Strauss or Gustav Mahler, but could he put that into words without sounding amateurish? He possessed neither the knowledge nor the vocabulary to express himself on a subject that meant at least as much to him as football league matches did to other people.

Nico had given Claudius what he wanted, youth and beauty, freshness and – perhaps not for long enough – insouciance, whereas all he had gotten from Claudius were obvious things from which they both profited although they cost plenty: dinners at the Restaurant Margaux, vacations in New York, a suit, a pair of shoes, a Tom Ford T-shirt. That was quite a lot, though nothing he couldn't have gone without. But whom had he met thanks to Claudius? Which singer, which pianist, which conductor of the many represented worldwide by Heinrich & Brutus and with whom Claudius consorted as easily as he did with his own mother?

There followed a car chase complete with roaring engines and screeching tires, and there was no doubt that it had been shot in San Francisco. The noise that assailed him from all directions became intolerable. He checked the time on his iPhone: ten past nine. He stood up, determined not to torture himself any longer. His attempt at self-distraction had failed. He should have known.

It was already dark outside when he emerged. He crossed Leipziger Strasse in the direction of Friedrichstrasse and looked around for somewhere to have a drink, preferably a bar, a darkened room with deep leather armchairs and a brass-trimmed teak counter − the kind of place you could find anywhere in New York provided you were in the right neighborhood. The watering hole he eventually entered was called simply "American Bar." It didn't exactly correspond to what he had imagined, but it would fulfill its purpose. He would be among people but alone. He looked around, sat down at one end of the almost deserted bar, and ordered a beer.

Lorenz

rau Bentz was beside herself, the housekeeper had announced, puce in the face, as she angrily surveyed those present. Her employer's indignation seemed to have transferred itself to her deputy, seamlessly and undiminished. Just imagine, that pianist, that, that – the name escaped her but Lorenz came to her assistance – "Olsberg, thank you," had stopped playing mid-recital, had broken off, stood up, and walked out, leaving the concertgoers to their own devices. And what now? What about the reception, the guests, the buffet?

What now? It was unlikely that Olsberg, who had made an unexpected, unaccountable exit and seemingly vanished without trace, would suddenly reappear. She was still awaiting a final decision, but if she knew Frau Bentz the whole function would be canceled because it would be positively absurd to hold a reception in honor of a guest who had offended the other guests in such a way. And she couldn't, knowing Frau Bentz as she did, imagine a reception without the guest of honor. That would be a party at which the invitees were either ignoring or consoling themselves for the fact that what ought to be happening wasn't. She was finding it hard not to get her sentences tangled up. She was, she repeated, awaiting another telephone call.

Silvio asked if the pianist's action had been politically motivated. Had he said anything along those lines? The housekeeper naturally had no knowledge of such a matter. She brushed the question aside with a dismissive gesture. "Frau Bentz mentioned nothing of the kind," she replied. "But I don't know, how should I? Politically motivated? Why? No, no, only an Italian would think of such a thing."

So saying, she turned on her heel and left the kitchen, in which the staff had congregated and were standing around irresolutely. What to do? Carry on? Clear away? Wait.

Ten minutes later, during which time she had again been on the phone in a distant room, the housekeeper, whose name no one seemed to know, reappeared in front of them and announced that Frau Bentz had decided to cancel the function altogether. No guest of honor, no reception. She had apparently contacted most of the invited guests – especially the most important ones like the Federal President and his wife, the Mayor of Berlin and his wife, Sir Simon and his wife, Frau Christiansen, and the foreign minister and his wife – either at the Philharmonie itself or via her cellphone. "She has most of their numbers. She knows them all."

She herself, said the housekeeper, would personally and politely turn away anyone ignorant of Frau Bentz's decision who appeared at the door. All preparations were to be canceled and arrangements regarding payment negotiated with the management of the catering service. They would be remunerated according to the work done. "That would be the fairest way."

"What do we do now?" said Silvio. "Clear away, for a start," Lorenz replied. He looked over at the Asian girl, who was steadfastly working away. She had evidently grasped what was to be done. Like a film running in reverse, she was packing up what had been unpacked in the last hour and a half. She smiled at him. He felt an irresistible urge to touch her.

Sophie and Klara

"That was really nice. A bit short, though," Klara said when they were standing outside. She might have been talking about a predictable change in the weather, for instance the drizzle that had set in before they emerged into the open. "Are we going home, then?" Her tone of inquiry could not disguise the fact that that was her dearest wish.

Sophie nodded at nothing because Klara wasn't looking at her. She suggested that they might go and have a drink somewhere, but she didn't know what to say when Klara said, "Okay, where?" She didn't know her way around this touristic desert. A bar? A café? The Sony Center? She was loath to risk a refusal, so they set off for the parking lot. They had left the Philharmonie without reencountering Solveig.

"Can you drive – I mean, in your condition?" Sophie spun around. What did she mean? Of course she knew what Klara meant. She was speechless, and she noticed she was swaying, but not because she was drunk, as Klara seemed to think, but because she felt as if the girl had punched her. In the chest. In the guts. How old should she have been before she could presume to say such a thing? There seemed no limit to their presumption. First her sister and now her daughter. The whole family. You think you can take any liberty, she thought, and before she could reflect on the matter and, after thinking for a moment, decide to say nothing as she always had, she said it softly but distinctly enough to be clearly understood:

"You really think you can get away with anything, you and your mother. You, your mother, and your stepfather, or whatever you call him – you're all the same. You treat the world as if you own it, only to destroy it."

She wondered what she meant herself, because she'd gone much further in speech than she ever did in her mind. Her lips uttered things she hadn't thought through.

Now it was Klara who said nothing because she probably hadn't reckoned with such furious opposition – because she hadn't expected any such offensive, indignant remark to issue from her naïve godmother's lips. And now this? What was wrong, what had happened?

Sophie walked on faster, purposefully, without knowing why, as if she had some objective. She had no objective, she simply wanted to get to her car. So she did have an objective, somewhere down in the Bellevuestrasse multistory. She only hoped she could find it again. She didn't remember which floor she'd parked her car on. How many floors were there, anyway? That was something she didn't have to share with anyone. The Seat, in which she could do as she pleased, was her property. She didn't care whether or not Klara managed to keep up with her. Eventually she broke into a run. She didn't care, either, if it looked like she was fleeing from the truth, fleeing from a girl who had misbehaved a bit. It might be a good thing if she got to the multistory and her car long before Klara. She might well drive off without her. She didn't care, it would even have been satisfying to sever the last tie that shackled her to her family, a tie that was nothing but a chain. Let Klara find her own way back to Zehlendorf, she was old and energetic enough. She didn't care what happened to the girl. She gave her imagination free rein. She went on walking, nobody called to her. It wasn't easy to find the way, which she only vaguely remembered, but she finally made it.

She spotted Klara from a long way off. The girl evidently had a better sense of direction than her. Only that could explain why she was already waiting for her beside the car. She wondered why her niece was apologizing to her.

"I'm sorry, Sophie, I'm sorry I behaved so badly, I haven't been feeling too good all day. It just slipped out. I didn't mean it to, really I didn't."

Sophie stared at her niece in surprise, wanting to say something, but what? She could already tell that something was happening which hadn't happened for a long time; something she couldn't suppress, something hidden deep inside her, was finding its way to the surface. She burst into tears. She started to weep, but since she didn't want Klara to see her tears she turned away, intending to open the driver's door. Instead, she thumped the roof of the car three, four, five times with the fist that was holding her keys, as if that little, impotent bird's claw could open something and release it just as she had just opened her eyes and released the tears, something embedded so deep inside her that no one would ever release it.

She felt Klara's hand on her shoulder. She smelled her faint perfume. How could it have escaped Klara that her aunt, whom she had never seen otherwise than self-composed, was weeping without restraint? It was impossible to conceal her present state of mind. Anyone seeing her would have noticed it. She turned around. She had nothing to lose. She wanted to say something reassuring, soothing.

But Klara had already started speaking. "You hate my mother because she stole your man. You loved Klaus. And you hate me too, because I'm there and I look on and do nothing. I can understand that. You're still in love with him. I can understand why you hate us, why you want nothing more to do with my mother, or with me either. But that you still love him – no, that I can't understand. Perhaps I can reassure you, though. The man she lives with, the man you love and who probably loved you too for a few weeks of his life, had another woman long before he took up with my mother. Mom doesn't know this, but I do."

She laughed. Before Sophie could say anything, she went on, "I know it best of all because it's me, because Klaus sleeps with me the way he would with any woman who comes near him and hints that it's okay, he can if he wants, she's available, she doesn't have anyone else right now. Do you understand? What did you expect of him? Another man would realize you're suffering and why, but not him. I'm young, that's my great advantage over you two warring sisters. Understand? No, you don't understand. I'm one of the ones he'd have cheated on you with if you were still together, at latest if I'd slept over at your place. If you'd been sharing an apartment he'd somehow have managed to sneak into my room at night – I'm eighteen, after all. He didn't try it on before I was eighteen, not that I'd have objected. You know him, you know there's something about him that makes him irresistible. To you, anyway, and my mother and me as well – must run in the family. It's embarrassing."

Sophie's tears had ebbed and dried before the first trickle reached her chin. Her anger, jealousy, and indignation had evaporated.

"I didn't know that. I thought you were completely clueless. I thought you were a naïve, innocent child, but you've a clear head and more common sense than I have. I'm not resentful. Maybe I should make it up with your mother."

The sudden change almost intoxicated her.

"Let's go. I'll drive you home."

Klara shivered. "You were right," she said, "I should have put on something warmer."

Esther

She paid the cabby, trod ankle-deep in a puddle, smothered a swearword in favor of a pained smile, shut the door, crossed the wet street, squeezed between two closely parked cars with her arms in the air, and opened the front door. The rickety elevator, whose sides briefly scraped the wall between the first and second floors, bore her slowly upward. Meanwhile, she inspected herself closely in the mirror. She tried to be as objective as possible, wanting to know what other people would have seen if they were standing beside her. As so often, she was happier with her appearance now than when leaving the apartment. That was probably because of the lighting, which had an amber tinge that lent her complexion a softness it lacked on other occasions. Strange, because the lighting was the same as it had been two hours earlier, when she'd found it less flattering. And she'd only drunk one glass of wine in the interim. She couldn't detect any clouding of her perceptions.

The elevator shuddered safely to a halt at the third floor. A problem for the residents' association, its shortcomings had been only marginally debated and then dropped again. She opened the apartment door, and since she couldn't hear the television she assumed that Thomas had already gone to bed or simply turned the sound down, the better to snooze on the sofa. She took off her thin, sodden shoes and massaged her cold feet. She didn't turn on the hall light, being able to find her way to the living room without it. She pushed the door open gently, so as not to startle him.

The television was off and Thomas wasn't lying on the sofa. This rather disappointed her. He hadn't expected her to be back so soon, of course. He'd expected that the concert would be of normal duration, and that she would go for a drink with Solveig afterward. She looked at the clock. It wasn't even ten.

How wise and farsighted she had been in 1996 to buy, on her father's advice, not only the third floor but also the attic and knock them into a duplex big enough to lose your way in, as Thomas liked to tell their guests. Among his periodic dreams was one of an apartment in which he lost his way even after living in it for years – an apartment in which he kept on discovering rooms of whose existence he was ignorant or whose existence he had forgotten, one of them the size of a ballroom with broken windows and birds unable to find their way out. It was a dream he dreamed regularly, because even though his desire for a big apartment in Sophienstrasse had been fulfilled, it was always possible to dream of one that was even bigger.

The bedrooms and the bathrooms – one for the parents and one for the children who didn't visit them as often as Esther would have liked – were on the top floor, which, seen from the inside, bore almost no resemblance to an attic. It had no sloping ceilings or mansard windows, no visible beams or skylights of any kind; on the contrary, it boasted a big enclosed terrace to which the architect had imparted the look of a "designer loggia," as Thomas liked to put it. And all perfectly insulated so you didn't start sweating even on hot summer days.

"Thomas?"

She wanted to check that he wasn't in the kitchen, but she wasn't sure her tentative cry would penetrate the kitchen door, so she opened it. It was dark inside, so she turned the light on. The neon tube above the stove flickered on and instantly steadied, discreetly illuminating the kitchen.

The half-full wine glass Thomas had drunk from was on the table. He had probably corked the bottle and put it in the refrigerator. His plate, beer glass, and cutlery were in one of the big twin sinks used mainly for washing hands and rinsing vegetables.

Thomas's rolled-up napkin lay beside the glass. It was his habit to fold and roll it up so that any stains were invisible. Lying on the table were the books she had left there weeks ago. She knew she would never read them. Books with white or dark blue dust jackets, they went especially well with the table designed in the fifties by Jean Prouvé, which bore the eloquent name Trapèze. The table had been inherited from Thomas's childless great uncle. It was by way of being the source of Thomas's good taste, he sometimes said, jokingly but not without pride.

She took a clean Burgundy glass from one of the upper kitchen cabinets and opened the refrigerator. She found the bottle without looking, she had only to bend down and feel for it. First came milk in a carton, then juices in plastic, and finally alcoholic drinks in bottles: white wine, champagne, aquavit. She hadn't expected the Cloudy Bay to be so cool. It was ice-cold, as if it had been waiting hours for her to drink it. She congratulated herself on the SMEG's efficiency. The expensive wines were kept in the wine cabinet, which was in one of the two pantries.

Having allowed the air to escape through the slit in the rubber stopper – it reminded her every time of the external urethral orifice, and thus of the fact that she would probably have completed her medical studies if she hadn't met Thomas, which she regarded as her life's biggest stroke of luck – she discovered that Thomas had drunk only a little, very little, almost nothing. One glass at most. Had he felt unwell? He hadn't complained of any discomfort. She didn't know how much he had eaten, or what.

She filled the big glass almost to the brim, not intending to return to the kitchen tonight. Once upstairs she wouldn't come down again. The Burgundy glass held nearly as much as two white wine glasses. That would be enough to give her a good night's sleep. She slept well not only after red wine, she slept even after drinking an espresso. She bent down again, gave the contents of the fridge a quick once-over, and removed two slices of San Daniele from their aluminum foil. She popped them straight into her mouth without any bread, because bread at night, tempting though it was, instantly turned into fat around the hips. The ham was cool and moist and stung her gums a little, probably because of the salt.

She shut the refrigerator door with her knee and left the kitchen. The ham fat on her fingers would leave imprints on the wine glass. She was just going out when she gave a start. The sound that had startled her was merely the fridge, whose motor had just started up with a gentle whoomph. There followed the deep, contented purr of a sleeping predator. The refrigerator was conveying how powerful and replete it was, like the belly of a well-fed lion. Esther felt as light as air.

The television was off, she needed only to turn out the lights, which she would do with one of the remote controls that lay strewn around everywhere, upstairs as well, of course. She was in no hurry, though, so she sat down on the sofa and surveyed the room. It presented her with a picture of materialized comfort. Property, beauty, culture, refinement. It was as simple as that to summarize what was so difficult to have and to hold, at least for many people: carpets, pictures, pieces of furniture. Most of them they had acquired only recently. Once the children left home they had boldly embarked on a kind of fresh start, had gone to Vitra in southern Germany and spent hours looking around in the showrooms for things designed to recalibrate their life, to lighten and redirect it toward carefree modernity. The only old friend was the sofa, which they had owned for twenty-seven years. Thomas had somehow managed to buy it out of the allowance his parents paid him to cover his college fees. A trifle unscrupulous of him, but he'd gone without other things to make up for it. Now, in spite of having financed their own children's education, they could afford anything.

That was what constituted her life: secure ownership, whose influence on a person's thinking could not be underestimated. She recognized its importance. Her life had paid off, and it wasn't over yet. Although it couldn't be said to have just begun, it was flowing peacefully downstream to the sea. She was happy. She was feeling more at home than ever. She deposited her glass on the Eames Elliptical table of which Thomas was so proud, stretched her arms out sideways, and made herself comfortable on the sofa.

When her right hand touched the Rataplan's cool leather it came into contact with some hard object that had no business there. Thomas's iPhone. It must have slipped out of his pocket while he was watching television. She yawned and put it in her pocket. She was tired. Thomas wouldn't miss it until tomorrow.

Olsberg's departure from the stage should have affected her more, but she had to admit that the nature of his unforeseen, theatrical exit had left her pretty cold. Perhaps it was the absence of any clue to what had prompted it. She hadn't the ghost of an idea as to what had driven him to act in that way, and she was pretty sure that applied to most people. Her lack of interest must have stemmed from the fact that the way the evening had turned out did not affect her life in the least. Her life took place elsewhere. The misfortunes of others – those who died in tsunamis or airplanes in places one never even contemplated visiting – were worth no more than a commiserative remark of which one knew, better than anyone, how insincere it was.

So why think about it? Had she stopped the cab and let him get in, her life might have taken a different course, but that she was neither prepared for nor intent on. She was thoroughly satisfied with what she possessed. Life wasn't like that. Her life lay elsewhere.

Her glass was half empty. That was enough. She would drink the rest upstairs.

She climbed the stairs, turned off the downstairs lights, and quietly opened the bedroom door. It was dark inside. Thomas had turned off all the lights. She felt ashamed of having waited so long before looking for him. He was ill, he must be feeling ill, she told herself as she groped for the switch of the floor lamp nearest the door, whose light would not disturb him.

Thomas wasn't there at all. She felt she had sensed that even before she turned the light on.

Lorenz

His urge to touch the Asian girl was at least as strong as his urge to speak with her, but not as strong as his desire to change the course of his life by doing something radical, a long-cherished dream that had so far failed to take definite shape. This house, Lorenz told himself, presented him with an opportunity to which he had never given any thought. He now considered it. This evening, tonight, he would grab it by the scruff of the neck. Never, he told himself, had his chances been better. It was quite simple. Everything here was eloquent of abundance, wealth, property, prosperity, luxury – the list of synonyms was endless. He listened. All the sounds he heard seemed familiar. He was waiting for silence and what would follow it.

The two chefs and the Asian girl were clearing up with the assistance of Silvio and Lorenz, who were careful not to get in their way. While the chefs and the Asian girl were calmly and impassively refilling the containers, cold boxes, and tubs with what they had calmly and impassively unpacked and distributed around the various working surfaces in the Bentzes' kitchen three hours ago, Silvio was displaying restlessness and haste. Lorenz remained outwardly calm. It was clear that the Italian's only thought was to get back to his family as soon as possible. No wonder, considering that this enthusiastically commenced but unsatisfactorily concluded night's work would earn him only a proportion of the fee he'd been expecting a few minutes earlier.

Lorenz had still not exchanged a word with the Asian girl. He didn't even know her name and was afraid that, yet again, this was as far as things would go. He repelled what attracted him before he had even considered making an advance. The shyness that barricaded itself behind his distant manner had long ago become a compulsive form of inhibition that rendered it impossible for him to behave like a normal or semi-normal person. If there had been someone he could talk to about it, his accursed shyness might have been exorcized long ago.

The Asian girl met his eye. She didn't evade his glances, she withstood them as if she would have no objection to him taking an interest in her. She was a head shorter and would have disappeared into his shadow if she'd been standing behind him, but she wasn't frightened of him. Rightly so, because there was nothing to be frightened of. Might that be why? Did she see through him? Was she looking at him without embarrassment because she knew there was nothing to be expected from him, let alone feared?

He made up his mind to ask for her phone number. She didn't look as if she had a boyfriend. She didn't look as if she would refuse to give him her number and possibly go out on a date with him. Or at least ask him for *his* number as to be able to call him on one of the days he usually spent at home on his own, like a neglected wallflower. Him, who was good-looking! Him, who could pass for a movie star! His pathological behavior must have a name. There had to be some medical term that encompassed all that filled him with envy of those whose lives differed from his own because they were free and easy. If there were a medical term there would also be a prospect of therapy. It wasn't just fear. It wasn't just shyness. He needed resources, money. He had none. That would now change. Money would improve his situation. A tropical island with Yui, Liu, Yoko, or whatever her name was. A date, a rendezvous, a trip. The Caribbean or something similar. An island in the Pacific.

He would call her when everything was over. He had a plan that simply must succeed, even though he didn't know how to carry it out. It wasn't a plan, actually, but an idea, though its method of execution kept eluding him. He would not be able to execute his plan until he was actually putting it into effect, if he did put it into effect. Only its implementation would create the requisite clarity in his mind and guide him step by step, so that everything went by itself. Not until he did what he had now decided to do – and he really had decided – would he find answers to all his questions and the right course to pursue so as to clear all the hurdles in his path. The decision was made; he would not depart from it.

It briefly occurred to him that this decision might only be an intensification of his dementia, but that thought soon gave way to another, contradictory but positively reassuring idea: the fulfillment of his plan would *cure* him of his dementia. And afterward, the Asian girl! The fulfillment of his plan would help him to call her and invite her out for a coffee or dinner at a restaurant, and he already knew which one: Borchardt.

He had a precise objective and a precise idea of what it looked like, but he still didn't know how he would actually get there. "Yes, just make a plan." Where had that song, that tune, that one line, come from? "Yes, just make a plan." He couldn't get it out of his head. He, who had once been such an excellent chess player that people had prophesied a great future for him – rightly so, he knew enough to know that; he who, like all brilliant chess players, had been able to think half a dozen or more moves ahead, had totally lost the ability to calculate what was to come. Retreat, hide, wait, pounce. He smiled and she smiled back. She smiled although he hadn't smiled on her account. But he had smiled. His decision was already having an effect. Her smile would bring him luck. It inundated him. He needed luck like anyone embarking on something they had never done before.

It would now have been simple to go over to her and ask her name, or ask if she had any plans for later on and whether she might care to go somewhere with him after work. That would have rescued this evening, but what about evenings in the future and the island to which he might be able to take her – her or possibly another girl? No, he was determined to remain in the house for as long as necessary.

Astrid

She was bedded down on a felty surface of some kind. It must be moss she was lying on. An aircraft engine was droning away in the distance. The sky was starlessly dark, but a ray of light was emanating from somewhere, possibly the lights of the aircraft traversing the gloom without illuminating more than fragments. The night was profoundly dark. Just that dull, distant sound and a modicum of light. Perhaps it wasn't an airplane but a helicopter far, far away. Astrid had been sound asleep, she didn't know where. She had no idea how she had gotten here, and where was here? It took a long time for memory to slowly return. Its sluggishness was soothing. Her state of exhaustion seemed to want to persist. Memory returned by fits and starts, lingering, taking one step forward, one backward. Pause. Darkness. Felty moss.

She hadn't imagined the light. It was still there when she opened her eyes again. She had probably gone back to sleep and was waking up once more.

It was hard to keep her eyes open, even though she wasn't really tired. She had no wish to move. If she moved the pain would return. That thought brought her back to reality. The tablet had worked. What remained of the pain, like an amorphous splinter, was the aero engine in the sky, in reality her body's fleeting recollection of the pain. She should think herself lucky, but she still wasn't out of the woods. First she had to stand up and look around. A perilous earthquake.

She still didn't know where she was, whether the darkness corresponded to the hour or whether it had been artificially created by closed shutters or drawn curtains. It all depended where she was. Japan, she thought, and saw a red ball on a white background. Was she still in Japan? A red ball. Sushi. Shimmering blue mackerel. Children in white smocks against a red background.

Japan eventually brought Berlin back. She was in Berlin, accompanying Marek Olsberg on his tour, lying on the double bed in her hotel room with the curtains drawn. In a moment she would know what time it was and get up. It would be time for the concert. Putting out her left hand, she made several vain attempts to locate her little travel alarm. She reached out still further. It wasn't there. Nor was the bedside table on which the alarm clock should have been standing. No bedside table or any other kind of surface. Her hand encountered nothing at all. She put out her other hand and touched a wall. The bed was a narrow one, not a double bed. She wasn't in her hotel room. It suddenly dawned on her where she was. Heavens alive, what time was it? The concert. She had fallen asleep in the dressing room and missed Olsberg's entry. The recital might have begun already. Being as considerate as he could be, Olsberg hadn't woken her when leaving his own dressing room to be greeted by the first applause of the evening. She would only have been a distraction. Applause! No, she'd heard no applause.

Careful not to make any hurried movements that might startle the beast, which had to remain pacified, she felt her forehead. It was as cold as the wall she had just touched and curiously similar in texture. What time was it? Slowly, she turned her head toward the door, the direction from which the light was coming.

A narrow strip, it came from Olsberg's dressing room at the end of the passage. The passage itself was in darkness. She slowly sat up in bed, but the beast did not stir. Rolling off the couch, she felt cold floor under her feet, felt for her shoes, hooked them toward her, and slipped them on without bending down because bending down was dangerous. They were comfortable suede shoes. Now came the crucial test: she had to stand up.

Either the migraine would recur at a stroke, or she was over it. She got up off the couch. She was over it.

She had sloughed off the pain like a snakeskin. The tingling in her hands was not unpleasant. Silence reigned. Olsberg had either turned off the loudspeaker in his dressing room or not turned it on at all. Out of consideration for her migraine he had left her to sleep in peace. She couldn't have done anything for him in any case. The droning sound was audible no longer.

She went out into the passage and pushed open the door of Marek's dressing room. The hands of her wristwatch stood at ten forty-five. The second hand was moving very fast, it seemed to her. She unstrapped the watch from her wrist and shook it like a thermometer, put it to her ear. The ticking was fast but regular. Ten forty-six. The recital was over. The watch was right.

Astrid noticed only then that Olsberg's overcoat was no longer hanging from its hook. She put out her hand. The recital was neither over nor still in progress. Where on earth was his coat? In its place was the empty garment bag and, on a hanger, the trousers, jacket, and shirt he'd worn before the concert with his shoes beneath them. Had he gone? She had obviously slept through the interval.

Eventually she turned on the loudspeaker connected to the auditorium. It crackled, she waited. Only a gentle hiss could be heard, nobody was playing the piano, nobody clapping, no sign of life. Did that mean the auditorium was deserted? Had everyone already gone home, and had she been forgotten? If so, where was Marek, who never forgot her? Marek never forgot her. She collected her few things together and set off for the concert platform. The wings were deserted but the emergency lighting was on. It probably remained on day and night. Her certainty that she had missed Olsberg's grand Berlin recital grew with every step she took. What she couldn't understand was his disappearance. It wasn't like him, knowing the state she was in, to leave her to her fate. Something extraordinary must have happened. The chair beside the door to the stage was deserted. She depressed the handle and opened the door. The big auditorium was in darkness. Only the emergency lighting was on. That was customary, she guessed.

Claudius

He hadn't exposed himself to another taxi ride but taken the subway to Charlottenburg. Not only on the way to Potsdamer Platz subway station but in the train itself and when changing to a streetcar, he had made several attempts to reach Marek on his cell phone, but without success. He hadn't expected anything else. Self-deception was a luxury Claudius allowed himself only in the non-professional sphere. He called the Adlon although he felt sure Marek wouldn't be there. Having him paged at one of the airports would have been not only pointless but absurd. Marek had no reason to respond to such a call, and it was extremely improbable, given his current situation, that he was thinking of traveling at all. Over the years – and tonight with a vengeance – he had amply demonstrated that he was his own lord and master. He owned apartments in London, Amsterdam, and New York, and he might well own country houses of which Claudius knew nothing. There certainly wouldn't be a flight to any of those cities at this hour, and it was unlikely that he would settle down to wait for the next one in some inhospitable Berlin airport departures hall.

Claudius simply couldn't think where to look for him. The city was big enough for someone to go to ground there for days.

Gradually, he began to entertain serious concerns – concerns that eclipsed his altercation with Nico, which he had temporarily but genuinely forgotten. It sickened him to imagine, one day in the immediate future, having to read in the newspaper that his client had not only cut short his Berlin recital but disappeared.

The media would not miss the chance of splashing such a headline.

Still more horrific, however, was the idea that a stranger might call to inform him or some other member of the agency, possibly even the receptionist, that Marek Olsberg had done himself a mischief. At best a detective, at worst someone from the press. Versatile Berlin presented suicides with plenty of opportunities and places in which to delay the discovery of their corpses for days or weeks on end.

Back home he tried to reach Astrid Maurer, but only her voicemail answered. She was protecting Marek, that was her job. He left a message without expecting a reply. He was ignorant of their relationship, of how close they were and how much she knew about her employer. Shielding him from the outside world was one of the tasks for which she was paid. She and Claudius had never become friendly.

A whiskey. He opened the bottle as soon as he'd removed his overcoat and jacket and draped them over a chair. He drank. He waited. What would have been nice now was a human voice, a hand or shoulder.

Sophie and Klara

They drove in silence. Then Sophie said, "See that place up ahead? Shall we stop?"

"Yes," said Klara.

"I'm sure it isn't a thing of beauty," said Sophie, "but if it's halfway decent it'll do me. How about you?"

Klara nodded. She was thinking, not of the fact that Sophie needed a drink but of the blissful feeling she'd always experienced in the old days, when she was little and her godmother had picked her up and indulged her with all the questionable treats that were either subject to restrictions or absolutely forbidden at home: candy bars, chips, Coke. She had unexpectedly taken a big step back into the past.

"Yes, let's go in," said Klara.

The café bar was called "Joy's Place." There was something contrived about its decor, something whose artificiality was not immediately noticeable. It had been modernized. The walls were bare, the upholstery wasn't chintzy, and the tables weren't covered with Formica, but the parquet floor still spoke the language of the days when the restaurant had been called "Ye Olde Times" or something similar. Not only that, but the menu hadn't changed: grilled Camembert, pan-fried sausages and potato salad, waffles and ice cream – all things that could be bought chilled or deep-frozen from a discount store. There was wine, however. The wine list featured a fair number of German wines.

There were few customers the twilit interior. Two tables were occupied by people conversing in low voices. The air smelled, not of tobacco smoke but of fresh, unventilated paint and – rather more strongly – of cooking fat used a dozen times over. It was a mixture that stung the nose, especially when compounded, or so it seemed to Sophie, with a soupçon of cat's piss or old-age incontinence, though the painters might simply have been too liberal with the ammonia. It was what Sophie and Klara had expected but not what they'd secretly hoped for.

After a mute exchange of glances they sat down at a table near the entrance, where they were almost entirely hidden from the other customers' gaze. After several minutes, during which they tried to attract attention by calling softly, a woman apppeared at their table. Very probably Joy in person, she smilingly took their order without a note pad. "Anything to eat?" She looked relieved when they said no. She probably wanted to close soon and go to bed or live it up elsewhere.

Klara ordered a glass of wine as well. Sophie brushed aside the thought that she was doing so only for her sake, not for pleasure but in order to reinforce, at least a little, the unexpected harmony that now reigned between them. Did a girl of her age really enjoy drinking, or was she doing so out of pity or solidarity, because lone drinkers are notoriously pathetic creatures whom it's advisable to handle with kid gloves?

"I get the feeling," said Sophie when they had clinked glasses and taken a first sip, "that we're among the last people to have heard Olsberg live. From now on there'll only be his recordings. Anyone who wants to hear him in the future will have the choice between two handfuls of CDs. That was his last, great moment."

She forbore to mention that she'd fallen asleep during the recital, and Klara gave no sign that this hadn't escaped her. It was unimportant.

"How long has it been going on with Klaus?" Sophie asked, discovering that it didn't hurt her to utter his name. Perhaps because she was worried.

"A few months."

"And your mother doesn't know?"

Klara shook her head.

"What if she did?"

"That would be awful. It would probably ruin everything. She doesn't know, though."

"How important to you is it, her happiness?"

Klara shrugged her shoulders. This briefly annoyed Sophie, but she drew a deep breath and restrained herself. Feeling compassion for her sister was inappropriate.

"Just give it up. It's bound to end in tears."

"I like him, I don't love him. He's…"

Sophie looked at her inquiringly. "He's what?"

"He's crazy about me. And he's" – she laughed – "better than nothing."

Sophie groaned softly. "Plenty's better than nothing," she said, "but something else is better than good. You're young, pretty, desirable. No wonder he likes you, you're a fount of youth. He must be fifty-six by now."

"Fifty-six, fifty-seven, no idea."

"Are you being careful?"

"What do you mean? We practice safe sex. He always uses a condom."

"I didn't mean that. That's a good thing, of course. I meant, won't your mother find out sooner or later?"

"No, we take care. She has her fixed working hours, as you know. She sticks to them and we know what they are. The earth would have to stand still before she changed them."

"What if you end it?"

"If I do, that'll be it. He'll suffer, but he'll suffer in silence. He won't leave her. Where would he go? He won't follow me if I leave."

"You're planning to leave?"

"I'm off to college next year."

"Do you realize what it means if a woman's own daughter has an affair with the man her mother lives with?"

"I try to think it's as dramatic as it probably is, but I can't. I seduced him, after all, not the other way around. He isn't really to blame for this state of affairs."

"He could have restrained himself."

"He could have, but you know self-control isn't his forte. Women don't like that."

"What do you know about women?"

"Not much, but enough."

"Has he ever talked about me?"

She could have lied, but she didn't. "No," she said, trying to evade Sophie's searching but inscrutable gaze. She didn't know how much Sophie could take.

"I'm glad you're telling me the truth. It's less hurtful than a lie you recognize for what it is."

"What do you think I should do?"

"Leave him to your mother and find yourself a boyfriend your own age, a nice young man but not one like him. He had his good qualities when he was younger, but he seems to have lost them."

"Who knows, I may have helped him to."

A dirty beer mat had been left on the table. Pensively, Klara waggled it in her hand. At length she made up her mind to speak. "Actually, he's at your mercy now."

"What?"

"You could blackmail him!" She laughed. "You could destroy this wonderful little family of ours. Wouldn't that give you satisfaction?"

"No."

"Just think. You call him, you speak in riddles, you drop a few hints, you meet with him in secret, and then tell him in detail what you know. Or you meet with my mother and tell *her* what you know. That would be explosive enough to blow the whole family sky-high. Bang, we're history."

Her laugh had taken on an unpleasant edge. Sophie found it no less surprising than her tasteless suggestion.

"Well, how does that appeal to you? Be honest, it's a tempting idea."

"It doesn't appeal in the least. It's a horrid idea, and I'd sooner you didn't even entertain such thoughts."

"So you'd sooner suffer in silence?"

"Maybe I'm not suffering at all."

"I don't believe that when I see you like this. Earlier on, in the garage? Everything'll have to come out someday, out into the open. The dirty linen, the pain inflicted on you. Everything needs airing and repairing."

"What makes you so sure? You're still far too young and I'm much too old. Some things can never be put right. I wouldn't even want them to be."

"You wouldn't like to see him again?"

"No. What for? He belongs to you now – for the moment. Do me a favor and get rid of him. The sooner the better."

"Really not?"

"Really not. Not anymore."

Sophie wondered whether to order another glass of wine. "No," she said, underlining her decision to lead a life from which any thought of that ludicrous Don Juan would be banished for evermore.

She smiled when she spotted Klara sneaking a look at her watch.

"You're right, it's late."

"It's half past ten."

"It's always either early or late, depending on your point of view. I'll drive you home and then myself. And then maybe I'll have a vodka." Abruptly, she went on, "I had a girlfriend in the States who claimed to suffer from an allergy to wine, which was why she drank nothing but vodka. Before meals, with them, and after them. During the day too, sometimes. Ah, poor Anna, how we used to laugh – about men among other things. She died so young. It can't have been the vodka."

"Who knows?"

"Yes, who knows? What does it matter how and why we die? We die, that's the main thing. There's no avoiding it."

Sophie paid the check and rose. They went outside. Sophie continued to talk of Anna, whom she had last seen nine years ago in Seattle. "Nine years ago, and it seems like only yesterday – as old folk tend to say." It may have been meant to sound bitter, but it also sounded conciliatory.

Anna had died four years ago without having seen her German friend again. She died far from her place of birth. "Bratislava or Brno – Brno, I think. Thanks to a good Samaritan she escaped death as an infant at her mother's breast, shortly before they got to Auschwitz. So what objection can there be to a few vodkas before the end that no one can defer in any case?"

Klara was staring at her aunt wide-eyed. She realized she knew nothing about her.

"Pff, what nonsense I'm talking."

"When shall we see each other again?"

"As soon as you feel like it," Sophie replied, opening the driver's door. "If you do, call me. If you don't, forget it. I'm here for you, anyway."

She tucked a stray strand of hair behind the ear of her grown-up niece, who was no longer a child but not yet a woman.

They got in. Sophie started the engine, engaged first gear, and drove off. While driving she started to hum to herself. Something by the Beatles, Klara thought, but she wasn't sure. Sophie could picture Anna so vividly, she all at once thought she could smell her and almost forgot about Klara. Klara shut her eyes, rather surprised by her aunt. Sophie was a stranger to her, really, and Klara was grateful to the alcohol for having loosened her tongue at least a little.

Esther

"Thomas?"

Of course Thomas wasn't in the bathroom, she would have heard him long ago, but she looked in there all the same. What else should she do? He wasn't there. She took a quick look in the mirror, left the light on and the door open. He must be somewhere, she told herself, but where exactly? Not in the apartment, anyway. He was out. Had she looked in the mirror? She couldn't remember. She thought of Solveig. Why of Solveig? She went back into the bedroom, where she sat down on the bed and tried to collect her thoughts, but all that occurred to her seemed to collect and explode in the center of her body. Her stomach went into spasm, and the spasm refused to subside. She needed to think. Olsberg. Solveig. She couldn't think. She sat staring into space. She thought of Thomas. No one else mattered. Her gaze followed the strictly geometrical pattern of the carpet and lingered on the strictly geometrical chair that stood on its edge, trying to establish a connection between carpet and chair and chair and carpet. How ridiculous! Her body was trembling. What on earth was she afraid of? It wasn't necessary to look at the clock to know that it was too late. Too late to go out. Thomas never went out on his own at this hour, not even with her. Something unforeseen must have happened. Had he left something he urgently needed at the hospital? She clutched at that straw. The straw afforded her no support, of course, it snapped and she fell through the ice. What could be so urgent? What could he have forgotten? A letter, a bill? Thomas never forgot anything.

Even if he had, it couldn't possibly be so important that he'd gone out without leaving a message. What had happened to him and why had she gone numb? Her dull sensation of overwhelming powerlessness gave way to one of banefully acute perceptivity. He had left the apartment long ago, that's what. He had gone out shortly after her. Perhaps he had, after all, left a message. She hadn't noticed because she hadn't been expecting one. It was unusual for them to write each other notes. I'm here, where are you? They nearly always discussed the day's agenda over breakfast: We'll meet at seven at such and such a place. If the situation changed there was always the phone.

She left the bedroom and went downstairs. She looked wherever something might be lying, in the hallway, in the kitchen, in the living room, on every table, on every working surface, in every likely and unlikely place, but she found nothing. Then she went upstairs again, turning out the lights on the lower floor, and paid another visit to the bathroom. She looked around as if compelled to search the same place again for some object she'd lost. He had left no message because he hadn't expected her to be back so soon, that was it.

She glanced at the mirror. No "Back soon, honey, kisses" written in lipstick. He'd even forgotten his iPhone, so she couldn't call him. He had left the apartment precipitately. Had something happened to the children? If something had happened to the children he would have tried to reach her by cell phone. By his iPhone. She felt for it. Together with an unused toothpick, she fished it out of the pocket of her blazer, which she still hadn't taken off. Recently, when they were having a Chinese meal, she had pocketed two toothpicks. The other one must have lodged in the seam. She unlocked the iPhone, which differed only negligibly from the preceding model, which she herself possessed. She had never opened his cell phone before. Never.

She hesitated for a moment. For a second or two, no more. His secrets, if he had any, lay open in front of her. She needed only to help herself. She didn't want to. The iPhone wasn't hers. She had never spied on him, never searched his pockets or his pocketbook, never had any reason to do so. Did she have one now?

The display glowed coldly. She hesitated before opening his messages. Her mouth was probably open, she told herself later, and her eyes would certainly have been open wide because she couldn't grasp, couldn't believe, the countless text messages she was reading and would have done better not to read because they weren't intended for her eyes or written for her lips to repeat; words that had never crossed her lips and would never do so. And they certainly weren't the fashionable expressions her children used to bring home from school and use there in spite of Esther's expostulations, but obscene turns of phrase, sometimes spelled out in full, sometimes abbreviated, but nearly always unequivocal. It was simply disgusting. And he had replied, echoing them with relish, or at least without embarrassment. No, these messages of varying length conveyed no shame. They were eloquent of unadulterated lust.

She was as unfamiliar with the person to whom most of the text messages were addressed as she was with the person who texted her several times a day. There was a yawning gap, a gulf as immeasurably deep as an alpine crevasse, between Esther and the unknown man and Esther and this stranger named Tommy, because the husband who owned this iPhone had never been called anything but Thomas. Not even Tom, as German youngsters called themselves these days. No, Thomas, only Thomas. This wasn't his iPhone. She must be wrong.

Of course it was his iPhone.

She didn't know any Tommy, far less any Sabine. Sabine? Sabine? She thought for a moment. Sabine wasn't an uncommon name, of course. It was quite common, in fact, but there was no one of that name in her circle of friends and acquaintances. The only Sabine she could think of was one of his medical technologists, and she had caught a glimpse of her on only two occasions because she seldom showed her face at the hospital. She wasn't the sort of doctor's wife who stuck her oar in, always knew better, and conveyed the impression that she was jealous of any skirt she wasn't wearing herself.

But what did it mean, the fact that she didn't know the woman? All it meant was that she had never wasted a thought on his potential infidelity. It meant that she was naïve and the other women could lull themselves into a sense of security. That was the whole point. That was the prerequisite for betrayal.

She read text message after text message, she read all he had written to this Sabine and neglected to delete, and what this Sabine had written to him, and what this Tommy, this stranger, hadn't deleted. A stranger in her bed. Sleeping with the enemy, the title of a movie she'd never seen. It was grotesque, but in view of these explicit, ambiguous, suggestive, equivocal, off-color, obscene, offensive messages her thoughts turned to Lady Di, whom she had never thought or spoken of except in derogatory terms, as a person responsible for her own misfortunes, which she was prepared to share with the world at large. That vapid young woman, now long dead, must have felt like her when she heard what her husband had said to his mistress on the phone, which had been monitored for all the world to hear: I'd like to be your tampon, the Prince of Wales had whispered to his beloved, never guessing that the whole world was listening and would thereafter be able to ridicule his deceived wife all the more knowingly.

While reading what the two strangers had written about the love they felt for one another, which excluded her because she was merely the wife, she realized that it wasn't about love but only about exchanging mutual assurances, couched in the most extravagant language, of the lust they felt for one another.

Esther flung the iPhone away as if it were a snake that had just bitten her, but the venom was already flowing through her veins and pervading her entire body. She stared at it lying on the bed, then reached for it again. Why should she tolerate this? She laughed, gulped down the lump in her throat, and deliberated. The doctor's wife may be naïve, she thought, but she isn't as stupid as the two of you imagine.

Lorenz

He had no need to close his eyes to see the Asian girl in front of him. The darkness around him was so complete, he couldn't see a thing. Except her. He now knew her name. He had finally plucked up courage and spoken to her and asked her what it was, less than an hour ago. He had bent over her and inhaled her scent like that of a flower. She smelled of carnations and nutmeg. "Sabrina," she said.

Her name was Sabrina — she pronounced it with a slight hesitation after the "b" and the "r" sounded almost English. Someone in her family must have seen the movie with Audrey Hepburn and Humphrey Bogart fifty or sixty years ago, when it was newly released. Sabrina could not be more than twenty-three. When he asked if he might call her, she'd told him her phone number without a moment's hesitation. Just like that, with a smile, uncomplicatedly. He had memorized it without her having to repeat it. It was like the old days: he had moved the central pawn, now the bishops could be developed.

Lorenz had hidden in a clothes closet, which was part of his plan. The time was now shortly after half past eleven. It was pitch-dark inside the closet. The house was a big, rambling establishment full of twists and turns, just as he'd imagined. It hadn't been difficult to avoid bumping into the housekeeper.

He had slipped away unnoticed. He knew that neither Silvio nor the housekeeper nor either of the chefs would wonder how he had managed it, still less miss him or credit him with what he planned to do: commit an illegal act. He was as unsuspicious as a poodle, he was harmless, and that made him invisible.

They might perhaps have said he was an oddball, which was a sufficient explanation for the behavior of a person in whom one wasn't interested. Yes, he was an oddball who disappeared off the face of the earth without an explanation and reappeared when no one was expecting. When he wasn't there no one thought of him – save possibly Sabrina, he ventured to hope.

It wasn't the first time he'd stood in a closet full of clothes. The other time was in an almost forgotten memory. It was warm in there, and he enjoyed the warmth. There was a smell of rose water and lavender. Having hidden in the same way as he had then, he was smelling the unfamiliar scents, the dry exhalations given off by the garments he was nestling against, slowly running his hands over the material and between the folds as if they could explore what lay beneath them when they clothed the body whose head had decided to wear them. The air was redolent of heavy perfume and fragrant soap and all those indescribable things for which words failed but not the images that flitted through his brain, some vivid and others indistinct. He knew the owner of all these clothes – and this certainly wasn't her only wardrobe – only from photographs that showed a woman younger than she was today. Verena Bentz was over sixty, in fact, but presumably still attractive. A *soignée*, imposing, alluring figure.

The memory that had eluded him until now concerned a closet in his childhood. He had hidden in it and waited for someone to discover him. It was a game.

Some boy or girl had counted up to fifty, leaning against a wall with their hands over their face, while everyone else scattered in all directions in search of hiding places in the house or garden in which they would sooner or later be discovered. He was ten or eleven at the time. Beate, the girl in whose parents' house they were, had taken absolutely ages to run him to earth. This long forgotten moment had unexpectedly resurfaced!

It certainly wasn't a hairdresser who had given Beate the pudding-basin haircut that emphasized her projecting ears and protuberant eyes. Children who didn't like Beate called her Frogface. She opened the wardrobe door and tried to kiss him, but he evaded her, turned his head away, and said, "That isn't part of the game." Then she let go of him, pushed him away, and locked the wardrobe door from the outside. He had misbehaved, but he didn't regret it.

He waited for someone to come looking for him, but he waited in vain. No one came looking. The cries of the other children, who had meantime ended the game of hide-and-seek in which he had long since ceased to play a part, grew steadily fainter and finally died away. He lost all sense of time.

He was compelled to release himself from the unfamiliar closet unaided, and brute force was the only answer. He hurled himself at the door with all his might until the wood splintered and gave way. Propelled from darkness into dazzling daylight, he fell headlong into the room. There was no sign of Beate. Although they attended the same school, he couldn't recall ever having seen her again.

Lorenz was naturally unarmed – he was no criminal, after all. He was as ignorant of where to obtain a gun as he was of how to use one. He wanted to change his life, that was all, admittedly by means which the end barely justified. All he needed was to avoid making mistakes and exercise a little imagination. He had to be agile and react quickly. The doorbell had been rung a few times by guests who hadn't attended the concert but wanted – in ignorance of the scandal – to pay their respects to the pianist, or by freeloaders who – without even wasting a thought on attending the concert – hadn't wanted to forgo the buffet. These disappointed visitors were gotten rid of by the housekeeper. However, silence had reigned for the last fifteen minutes. No cars, no doorbell. He had been waiting for half an hour. Sabrina, the chefs, and Silvio had left the house long ago. The hosts, who had been robbed of their soirée by the pianist's scandalous behavior, would be returning home any minute.

The wardrobe door was only ajar. Lorenz gently pushed it open and tiptoed out into the room, though tiptoeing was quite unnecessary because the parquet floor consisted of solid wood and didn't creak. The firmness of the floor gave him a feeling of safety and stability. In the bathroom, which he had yet to set foot in, he expected to find marble or granite, a cold material.

In the kitchen he had appropriated a flashlight he saw lying in a drawer, proof if necessary that his forthcoming robbery had been spontaneous, not planned. The idea hadn't occurred to him until the evening had taken an unexpected turn. His robbery was a result of Olsberg's unforeseen exit.

The venture would have been too dangerous, and consequently doomed to fail, if he'd had to grope his way around blindly in total darkness. The beam of the flashlight in his outstretched hand traveled across a big bed that could only belong to the lady of the house, because all the objects and pieces of furniture betokened a woman who spent a lot of time in this spacious room. Over the bed was a colorful Japanese woodcut, a blue ship against a dark sky, too difficult to remove from its frame, probably valuable, and certainly no copy. The risk of damaging and devaluing the sheet by rolling it up was too great. Damaging valuable objects for no good reason was not his intention.

He was unaccustomed to making his way around strange houses in a free and easy manner, not being an experienced burglar. He wasn't a burglar at all, strictly speaking. He hadn't effected a forcible entry. They had opened the door and invited him into the house. He hadn't left it, that was all. No skeleton key or glass cutter had been necessary, nor would he have known how to use them. He had already been in the house before it occurred to him to look around and take what seemed valuable enough to be sold later on. Helping oneself to things, that was the correct expression. Who to sell them to was something he could worry about later. On television and at the movies, thieves always knew where to find fences who would buy the stuff they'd stolen. He shone the beam on a chest of drawers and cautiously opened the uppermost drawer. It was easier than he expected. It glided toward him like something on rails.

It was full of jewelry. Full of opulence. Lorenz had not been prepared to succeed so quickly. Everything was going like clockwork. He wasn't an expert, but he felt convinced that these stones could only be genuine. Genuine and as valuable as the woodcut hanging on the wall, which he had left to itself. How could it be otherwise in view of the wealth with which this house was impregnated?

He gathered all the pieces together and slid them carefully into one of the two plastic bags he'd stuffed in his pockets before leaving the kitchen. He opened the second drawer, which contained nothing but underwear. The third held stockings and the fourth was empty, or apparently so. To make quite sure Lorenz crouched down and felt around inside it. His fingers touched paper. Reaching into the drawer, he brought out a bulging envelope and shone the beam of the flashlight on it. His hands were trembling. The envelope had been stuck down and torn open, so something had already been removed from it.

His assumption was correct. The contents weren't letters, they were money − money that had possibly been long forgotten. He took it out. It was all in 500 euro bills − thirty of them or more, he estimated, possibly forty or fifty. What an incredible stroke of luck, what an unexpected fortuity! The money might have been lying there waiting for him. It ought to be enough to make Sabrina happy and guarantee him the change of life he needed. Yes, it was enough. Enough to make him happy. Not being a gambler or an addict, he would content himself with that.

Astrid

She tried to reach Verena Bentz, but she didn't answer. Her cellphone ringtone was probably too quiet to drown the noise of the guests crowding around her and Olsberg at her house. Astrid hadn't noted or stored her land line number. She tried Olsberg, but immediately triggered his cellphone answering device, the familiar female voice that spoke English and made a rather elderly impression. She didn't wait or leave a message. Marek wouldn't listen to it tonight in any case. He had either left his cellphone turned off on purpose or, which was more likely, forgotten it after the concert.

Astrid, who seldom had to rely on her ill-developed sense of direction, looked around her. She had no idea which way to go. It was so dark in many places that she had to take care not to trip.

It was almost miraculous that she ultimately, in a very short time, found herself standing outside without having passed the porter. She had blindly but unerringly obeyed a vague feeling, and the decision had paid off. She had opened a door that gave onto a deserted, dimly-lit staircase. Her heels clicked on the stone floor. Lightly holding the handrail, she descended the stairs without haste. She was still unable to grasp that her migraine had subsided. Fear of never getting rid of the pain was one of the many symptoms to which one was prone during an attack.

She had tried two doors on the assumption that they led outside. The first was locked; the second, which was one floor lower, had actually opened. It was drizzling.

She walked across the parking lot and looked back. The open space outside the stage door was deserted. No one was lining up for an autograph, no fans, no friends one hadn't been expecting but who were always to be reckoned with in a city like Berlin. Unlike the stage door, the main entrance was in darkness. For a moment she considered going and asking the porter if and when he had seen Olsberg. Verena Bentz and her chauffeur had presumably been waiting for him, possibly in company with Friedrich Franz Bentz, whom Astrid hadn't met, the immensely wealthy owner of a gardening tools empire. At that moment a taxi came down the street, and since she had no umbrella with her and was getting cold, and it would be a while before another taxi came along, she hailed it. Although she was on her own and nothing and no one was compelling her to do anything, she had a nasty feeling she was acting precipitately. But she wasn't. She gave the cabby the address in Potsdam, which she had memorized, and he drove off. The taxi was warm and did not smell of stale tobacco smoke.

"How long will it take?"

"Half an hour," said the cabby.

Almost exactly thirty minutes later, having neither speeded nor dawdled along the Avus and later along streets flanked by gates behind which mansions stood in grounds spacious enough to be justifiably described as parks, they pulled up outside the house in which the big party in honor of Marek Olsberg's Berlin concert had been due to take place. That it wasn't taking place dawned on Astrid the moment she noticed the absence of parked cars. Few lights were visible inside the house. Somewhere, a light came on and went off, and she thought she saw the beam of a flashlight flit across the window pane. She noticed it, nothing more.

She wondered if she'd given the cabby the right address, an idea in conflict with her better judgment. It certainly was the right address, but — just as certainly — not the right time. It lacked all that would have made it the right time: luxury limos, politicos' bodyguards, open doors, open windows, lights, glitz and glamor, a catering service's van, people smoking and chatting on the stretch of gravel outside the big front door, evening gowns, the clink of champagne glasses, cries of bravo, clapping. She bent her head a little for a better view of the house. It looked rather different by night than it had in daylight. On the other hand, the big houses in this district all looked much the same. She had seen enough, though. This was undoubtedly the Bentz place. She asked the cabby to wait and felt in her purse for the slip of paper on which she'd noted down the address.

It was the right address.

"It's the right address, but something's wrong," she said quite softly. It didn't matter if the driver failed to catch what she was saying, all that mattered was to attract his attention in some way.

"Please wait for me."

"How long will you be?"

"Just a minute or two. I'll ring the doorbell and come straight back."

He yawned and shrugged, making no move to open the door for her, not that she'd expected him to.

Nor had she expected the iron gate to open so easily. She didn't have to ring the bell for it to open. It swung open at her touch as if some invisible mechanism had sensed the presence of a visitor, as perhaps it had.

She hurried toward the house along the gravel drive and climbed the broad flight of four steps, which was flanked by olive trees in massive urns. The taxi waited with engine idling and headlights dipped.

As if she'd been expected, the door opened just as she was about to press the bell with her forefinger. She recognized the woman she'd already seen that afternoon, the one who ran the Bentzes' household.

She gave Astrid a cool reception and put her in the picture at once, having expressed surprise that she didn't know what had happened.

Astrid froze, aghast. It was only a few seconds before the unimaginable information became transformed into a kaleidoscopic idea that splintered and dispersed in all directions.

In a flash, her migraine returned. She asked the housekeeper to explain the situation once more, she was so utterly surprised and disconcerted, whereupon the woman's face assumed an extremely ill-tempered, almost malign expression, for all the world as if Astrid were also to blame for the incident that had affected so many people, not least the housekeeper herself and her domain. Still striving to take in what she was being told, Astrid pressed both palms to her temples. The pain was unbearable.

Incapable of getting a word out, she clung to the doorframe for support. The housekeeper made absolutely no move to invite her inside. Desperately, Astrid strove to recall her name but failed. She'd forgotten it.

"I knew nothing about this. It's the first time I've heard about it. I heard nothing, I was asleep. I had a migraine, and it's coming back."

"I'm very sorry," said the housekeeper, unmoved, "but you and your piano player will have to live with what happened. At all events, the party's canceled. All that work was wasted. Well, there are worse things, an earthquake or a tsunami, for instance. Compared to that, we've gotten away with a black eye."

She seemed to brighten a little at her joke, so she grinned as she firmly shut the door after saying goodbye to Astrid without asking if she wanted a glass of water. A glass of water was just what she wanted. That and that alone. She staggered back to the taxi, so dazed that she didn't even notice the cabby's worried expression.

"Everything okay?"

"Do you have any water? I need to take a tablet."

"Water? No, all I have is some beer."

Esther

She wasn't technologically gifted, but she wasn't a total ignoramus either. Although there might have been a simpler way of attaining her objective, she chose one that required no lengthy deliberation and no elaborate phone call to her son, who would have explained things that generally sounded more complicated than they actually were. Once her idea had matured, the consequent deliberations followed automatically. They lined up like a string of black pearls on an invisible thread. She had devised a neat, insidious plan. If she didn't put it into effect now she would regret it later. She might regret later if she *did* put it into effect now, but she didn't care. The feeling that she was indulging in a petty, embarrassing act of revenge did her good. It took her mind off the worry of thinking ahead. What would happen tomorrow? Was this the end of her marriage? No, she didn't want to think about that.

She selected two dozen of the text messages sent by Thomas to Sabine and Sabine to Thomas, or Tommy to Sabine and Sabine to Tommy, or Your Stallion to His Mare or Your Mare to Her Stallion. She would give Thomas as nasty a surprise with his undeleted messages as he had given her – unless "nasty" wasn't utterly inappropriate and she ought to find a more suitable word.

In her study two minutes later, she lifted the silver-gray, aluminum lid of her wafer-thin laptop and turned it on.

Her inbox contained twenty-three forwarded text messages from Thomas's iPhone. Twenty-three proofs of what he was capable of and what she, in her naïvety, had thought him

*in*capable of. She opened the emails. There they were in black
and white, complete with the usual abbreviations and graphic
Internet slang – a phallic 8====>, for instance – as well as
errors of haste and transmission. Here and there umlauts had
been transformed into Greek characters and paragraph breaks
substituted for interrogation marks. Several of the messages
had broken off in midsentence, probably because of her.
Esther pictured herself entering whichever room Thomas had
happened to be composing an SMS in – their bedroom or the
bathroom, for example – hence the truncation of his intimate
correspondence with Sabine. Why he hadn't immediately
deleted the messages that passed between them remained a
mystery to her. She saw herself walking into the bedroom or
bathroom and giving him a kiss. He would meantime have
slipped the iPhone into his pocket.

The longer the messages, the more explosive the material
they contained. They ought to make a nice, readable little
sheaf, neither too thick nor too thin. Thomas would have
plenty to sink his teeth in, chew, and digest. She thought for a
moment. She needed some decent paper. The coldblooded way
in which she was acting surprised her; it was an unexpected
accretion. She remembered some good paper and found a
packet of handmade, watermarked sheets in one of the bottom
drawers of her desk. It had been a gift from the children – not
Thomas – years ago, but she had never used any because she'd
never had occasion to write a formal letter.

She had heard that necessity is the mother of invention
without ever experiencing it in person. She hadn't expected a
thirst for revenge to demonstrate the truth of it, even though it
was obvious. She knew she was driven by vengeance. Love had
given way to retaliation, the quiver from which she was now
firing poisoned arrows.

She printed out twenty-three messages. The matt sheets slid
through the printer like silk. She ended up with eight sheets of
handmade paper printed on one side only. A nice little batch.
If she'd had more time at her disposal at a different time of day,
she would have gone to a copy shop or printer's and had it

neatly bound. Unfortunately, that wasn't feasible at this hour of the night. She might previously have underlined the unsightly spelling mistakes.

The sheets looked as pretty and seductive as a gift no one was expecting, certainly not at this hour. It was neither pretty nor seductive, even if its contents dealt with seduction.

She looked at her watch. When had she said she'd be back? It was now twenty past ten. Concerts generally lasted until shortly before ten, often somewhat longer, depending on the audience's emotional state and the length of the encores. She had once heard a pianist dissatisfied with his performance repeat an entire suite, to the subdued annoyance of those who really wanted to go home and the loudly expressed delight of others who couldn't get enough of him. However, no classical recital in the world that had begun at eight went on beyond a quarter to eleven.

Thomas would be home soon, even though he could – if all went well – count on her not being back before midnight. After all, she had to take care of poor, deserted Solveig. Thomas could rest assured that they would eat in some familiar restaurant or other, have a couple of drinks, and chew the fat. At that moment her iPhone rang so unexpectedly that she gave a jump.

She answered. It was Thomas. She had a few seconds in which to pull herself together, because he spoke first. Holding her breath, she tried to imagine where he was – a subject on which she had wasted no thought until that moment. She tried to pretend she was in a public place. She was trembling. She would begin by saying that it was very noisy, she could hardly understand him.

He casually inquired if the concert was over. "What?" she said. "I can hardly understand you!" He repeated his question and she replied in the affirmative. "It's just finished. It's terribly noisy, I can hardly understand you!" She was lying just as he was, except that their lies reposed on different foundations. He asked how it had gone. "The recital, you mean? Fantastic!"

That his interest in her answer was rather scant, as scant as his interest in classical music in general, would not have surprised her even if she'd really been where he supposed, and if he'd really been where he convincingly pretended to be, except that this time she knew better. He couldn't – for the first time for how long? – hoodwink her tonight. She couldn't tell what phone he was calling her on, probably the woman's landline. What was her name again? She could have asked him now. She would simply have been able inquire – casually – what his medical technologist's name was, saying that Solveig had just asked her. Instead she repeated that the recital had been truly fantastic, absolutely unique. She mustn't arouse his suspicions at any price; he must be unwitting, lulled into a false sense of security. The soft pillow he rested his head on was her gullibility, the classical bedding of the deceived wife.

She almost said "Take your time" but restrained herself. "Where are you?" she asked innocently, but instead of saying "In bed" or "In the kitchen" he replied, "At home. At home."

"Yes, that I'm aware of," she said with a laugh, almost triumphantly. It did her good to torment him a little. It was liberating, but she noticed that it failed to help her shake off the burden that weighed her down. She still hadn't grasped what the betrayal whose victim she was would have in the way of consequences. She knew only that those consequences were inevitable. She could feel them all over her body, but how to deal with them? She wasn't tormenting him, she was tormenting herself.

It must have set his nerves jangling when she casually mentioned that she was feeling tired and Solveig even more so – "Aren't you, Solveig?" – because Olsberg had played an exacting program that had demanded extreme concentration from the audience, and then, out of the blue, announced that they were going to take a taxi together and go home.

"I'll drop Solveig at her place and be home in twenty or twenty-five minutes. Are you in bed already?"

"No, not yet, I was just going to— "

"You've no need to wait up. Go to bed."

"Of course I'll wait up. I must get—" He broke off. He almost said "going," thought Esther, but he suppressed it and swiftly substituted "get myself something to eat. See you soon, darling. Are you hungry too?"

She ignored the question and said casually, "See you." She couldn't bring herself to utter a "darling." She had laid her "darling" in chains.

The conversation was over. He hadn't smelled a rat. He still thought her as stupid and unsuspecting as she had been hitherto. Easily fooled, effortlessly deceived and betrayed. Until tonight, he'd been able to rely on pulling it off.

Even while thinking about him, however, she realized that this had been the last time they'd talked in a seemingly unconstrained manner, like a married couple confident of each other's fidelity. Tonight's rift heralded years of tribulation, aging, bitterness, withdrawal, uncertainty, and regret. For her, not for him. He would be facing a secure future and a peaceful old age with his Sabine – or was it Susanne? The woman might leave him someday, but Esther wouldn't even hear about it. And even if she did, it would be poor consolation at the end of a long journey together and a parting no one had expected – not even he, presumably – on this night she would remember for the rest of her life.

No wonder she suddenly burst into tears. Was there anything she could call her own after investing all that belonged to her in this marriage? Perhaps too little. Probably too much. Any interest she had earned would not add up to a happy life. Why was she thinking like this, in terms of capital and dividends, profit and loss? How could she think of anything at all at this moment? Her thoughts were clear and chaotic at the same time. She saw herself fumbling with a knife but couldn't drive it home. She was defenseless. He had poisoned her tonight. She would never touch him again.

She heard herself saying, "Poisoned forever."

So it actually happened, what you read in many books and what she had always regarded as trite, inane verbiage: you spoke without meaning to and could hear yourself speak. The pain lodged deep inside her had overflowed her lips. Beyond the impregnable armor stood a person that bore resemblances to her and listened to her like a stranger whispering to herself, "Poisoned forever."

What if she continued to display a semblance of cluelessness and simply destroyed the printouts instead of brandishing them under his nose?

Wasn't that a tempting alternative to the head-on crash that would inevitably result if she really did continue along the road she had taken by printing out these tell-tale text messages?

She could still grab hold of that sheet anchor, which would be more helpful than the abrupt end of their model marriage. Wasn't she capable of doing that? She could still change course, but in order to do so she would have to get out of here. She couldn't be found in their apartment, she should be in a taxi on her way home. Thomas would learn that the concert had ended prematurely but she hadn't told him so on the phone. She would find some explanation for that. His relief that she hadn't gotten home before him, so she hadn't noticed his absence, would dispel his misgivings. She wavered between two very different alternatives: either keep silent as if she knew nothing and leave the mendacity to him, or reveal what she knew tonight. All she had to do in the latter case was implement the plan she'd thought so original, so hilariously funny. It was original beyond a doubt, but she was beginning to doubt if it was really as hilariously funny as she'd originally thought.

What she was holding in her hands was irrefutable evidence that would end not only her marriage but also her future. She wouldn't be able to live like that. Or would she? Would she be able to live like Solveig? The next time she went to the Philharmonie, would she so as a deserted wife arm in arm with her friend, the unenviable woman who dreamed of socially inferior hairdressers?

She eyed the sheaf of paper in her hand. The pressure of her fingers had creased it a little. Time began to speed by. Not having smoked for over twenty years, she was itching for a cigarette.

Those sheets contained a part of the truth but not all of it. She tried to look at them as Thomas would look at them in a minute if she handed them over, but her own viewpoint was colored by a despair he would be bound not to share. He would be shocked by his stupidity but he wouldn't feel guilty, or only a little. They weren't on the same emotional track. He could live with them both, with her and his girlfriend.

She would hand him the wretched sheaf of paper with the words, "Here, a present for you. It contains plenty of nice surprises. Sensuality, eroticism, sex – everything a man could desire." She could say it with a smile or a hint of irony. That would still further reinforce the impact of the first message when he read it – uncomprehendingly at first, then shocked at his own words and the fact that they'd been discovered because he hadn't deleted them. If he had been standing in front of her at that moment she would have hit him. In the stomach and the face, and, if he turned his back, in the back.

Never had she found it so difficult to come to a decision, but time was running out. She looked at her watch. Soon. Perhaps it would also be quite easy not to decide at all – to destroy or hide the printouts, put his iPhone back where she'd found it, leave the apartment, and make a second arrival by taxi in three quarters of an hour.

Johannes

His leave-taking from Bettina alias Marina had been as cool as if they were strangers, which indeed they were. Any additional word would have been a word too much, any physical contact an invasion of the privacy to which she had just granted him access. She hadn't had to fend him off by force; a glance – not even a movement – had sufficed. What was it she now needed to protect herself from? Surely not the danger that he would tell his best friend about his encounter with the latter's daughter? The thought of doing so was unendurable. He wouldn't have done that even to an enemy.

He couldn't seriously have expected anything other than resistance and coldness, even if he had wanted something else. He knew from experience that reality always had a flip side as palpable as the one you could see. Except that it remained invisible even when you'd perceived it.

No handshake, no friendly gaze. They had faced each other feeling at a loss.

He had no need to look at his watch to know that it would soon be midnight here. With evening only just beginning elsewhere, it was now time to call Renate. Yesterday – or the day before? – he had called from New York at this hour. There were certain rules and principles in his life to which he strictly adhered, but which he never spoke about with anyone. It was enough that those to whom they applied were aware of them, and they included Renate. Among these rules was the daily phone call, the daily conversation spanning hundreds or thousands of miles; likewise fidelity to his wife, which did not preclude straying from it, and the fact that he seldom worried what Renate thought of him or what she knew, a comfortable state of affairs he left it to others to assess.

Now that Marina had gone, a faint residue of her perfume lingered on his body, on the pillow, and on the rumpled bedclothes he now pulled over himself. He would take a shower and the memory of her body would soon begin to fade. He failed to make sense of tonight's experience. He couldn't rid himself of the dismaying sensation that he'd made a mistake. What mistake? He would have liked to discuss it with someone, but he couldn't. He would have liked to turn the clock back, but he couldn't. With the help of a therapist? He didn't know any therapists.

Before he could call Renate he was overcome by sleep.

#

It was already getting light when he awoke, and his memory of the previous night had faded a little. The less he thought about it the quicker it would be forgotten, even when he was face to face again with Bettina's father. A vestige of her perfume still lingered.

It was shortly after seven. His flight was scheduled to leave Tegel at 11:35. He had no need to hurry, but he was glad to have a deadline to meet. He showered and shaved in that order, as usual. He concentrated on himself so as to think of nothing else, which he didn't find difficult.

He was wide awake and chipper when Renate took his call. He told her about the impressive concert he'd heard at the Philharmonie and said he hadn't called because he'd fallen asleep. What he told her differed not at all from what he usually told her no matter where he was, whether in Berlin or in New York.

"How lovely. A concert! Who was playing?" she asked. He wasn't prepared for that question but remembered that a pianist was involved. He was still searching around for the name when she said it. Renate had a phenomenal memory.

"Marek Olsberg?" she asked.

"Yes. Wonderful. A fantastic pianist."

"Yes, I've heard of him," said Renate, without adding what she had just heard on the radio: that the internationally celebrated pianist Marek Olsberg had discontinued his recital at the Berlin Philharmonie just before the interval and had not resumed it.

"And?"

"If he ever plays in Düsseldorf we'll go together, I promise. You ought to hear the man. He's simply amazing."

"Yes, I know, of course. But I don't think he'll ever play in Düsseldorf."

"No? Maybe in Cologne, then," he said, and they changed the subject as casually as they had broached it.

It wasn't until later, in the airplane, that he read a newspaper report of what had happened and what he'd naturally been in total ignorance of. And it wasn't until he started to read that he thought of Renate – too late, whichever way one looked at it.

Perhaps she'd known more than she was prepared to admit. It was quite possible that she'd already heard what had happened when they spoke on the phone. If so, how well and convincingly she had lied! And if she had, how hard or how easy had she found it? Why had she lied if she did? What was the truth?

He felt caught out. He started to sweat. Had she found it easier to lie than admit what she knew? Was she protecting herself by protecting him, or was she protecting him wittingly and defenselessly? What secret pleasure did it give her to hear him talking away like mad, not even realizing that, in order to remain credible, he should have done precisely that? He felt caught out like a little boy. A poser. A cheat, a con man. A fraud. She had deliberately coaxed him out onto thin ice. She had realized that he didn't know what had happened when she asked about the concert. He had mentioned it first, not her. Being quick-witted, she had then submitted him to a test. Relying on the fact that he would someday guess her secret without being able to react, she could now celebrate a triumph. Now what?

He didn't know. Had he seen the newspaper sooner, he would have told her what she already knew and she would have had no choice but to believe him. It would never have occurred to her to mistrust him. How stupid and incautious he'd been. If he had said he'd gone to bed early because he'd drunk too much, he wouldn't have given Renate any cause for suspicion.

It was too late to put things right by shedding a different light on them. Could he, as if he'd been present, come home and tell her about the unexpected incident that had upset the concertgoers at the Philharmonie and given risen to wild speculation, or was his only recourse to say nothing and hope that she wouldn't raise the subject again? If she wanted to torment him a little, she would mention the concert again tonight over dinner in a restaurant, or tomorrow at breakfast, or later, perhaps, in the presence of a third party. She could also put on one of Marek Olsberg's CD's without a word and relish the thought of what was going on inside him as he pretended not to notice what was being played.

At the same time, he knew of no one more magnanimous than his Renate – "my Renate," as he always called her to his friends.

He ordered a coffee although, having acquired a considerable knowledge of coffee-growing thanks to his predilection for good coffee, he abhorred airline coffee no matter which airline served it. He would have preferred a whiskey. It would at all events have been better suited to his time of ignominy than the lukewarm, sourish beverage about to be brought him, which he would, after the first sip, send back with a look of revulsion. A whiskey would be nice now, he thought, but alcohol was inappropriate at this time of day.

He must at least try. There was a glimmer of hope that Renate knew nothing, and that he had only imagined everything that had been going through his head. On coming home he would tell her what he had read as if he had witnessed it himself. Since he possessed no program, he would check what Olsberg had played on the Internet. He would describe how Marek Olsberg had stood up and walked out mid-recital. He read on.

More information about his reasons and his future plans would probably emerge later, but by that time only a few fans would be interested.

His coffee arrived promptly, and he drank it after all. It tasted better than he had expected. It was hot but not too hot. Olsberg and Marina now formed a couple in his mind, with himself standing between them. Their behavior remained a mystery to him.

These thoughts had almost made him forget his annoyance with the hotel staff, who had, when he checked out, hit him with a fine of 150 euros for smoking in a nonsmoking room. He learned that he hadn't been betrayed by the smoke alarm, which reacted only to extreme heat, not smoke, but by the educated nose of the relevant chambermaid, who had reported what she'd smelled to reception before Johannes got to the lobby to pay his bill. Once his attention had been drawn to the fact that he had personally signed the arrival form warning hotel guests of this penalty, he'd had no choice but to debit his credit card with a sum only a trifle smaller than the price of the room.

Lorenz

Something fell to the floor and smashed to smithereens. Lorenz had no idea what it was. He hadn't touched or bumped into anything. What now? What had transformed itself into a mound of shards in the space of half a breath? A vase, an empty aquarium, a big bottle of perfume? Not a small object, at any rate. His clumsiness must have alerted the entire household. It was impossible that the door wouldn't burst open at any moment, that someone wouldn't come to check on the source of the noise. Their suspicions would have been aroused and Lorenz had led them straight to him, so he hid behind a curtain and waited, aware of the risk that he might be seen from the partially illuminated street – if someone actually paused and looked up.

He waited with sweat streaming down his back. He had never sweated so profusely. But nobody came. The noise he'd made was followed by the same silence that had reigned before. All he heard was himself, his breathing, his footsteps. The house was evidently so well insulated that its occupants, uninvited guests like himself included, could do as they pleased without being heard. No footsteps save his own, no doors slamming, no voices. Everyone appeared to have gone to bed. On the other hand, the owners weren't back yet.

Absolutely no one had heard him, at least, and even if a distant sound had carried to their ears, they hadn't credited it with the significance it merited. Lorenz directed the beam of the flashlight, which had already lost some of its power, at the floor. The fragments belonged, not to a vase or an aquarium but to a glass bird readily identifiable by its pouched beak, which was intact, as a pelican. The rest was unrecognizable, smashed, and worthless. It had undoubtedly been a valuable object. Something from a different era – something people like the Bentzes could easily afford. Lalique, wasn't that the name of these glass antiques? Then again, what did it matter what they were called?

His plastic bags were well filled but not to the brim. Well filled and moderately heavy – heavy enough for him to have to take care they didn't tear. That would have made a noise compared to which the sound of the breaking glass had been innocuous.

He might not be rich, but he had – within half an hour – become far better off than before. He now had enough money to live on for months, possibly years. He had no debts to settle, he could spend the money. He was fancy-free for the first time in his life. He could also invest it. There were plenty of opportunities to capitalize on a quick profit but most of them were associated with risks he was unwilling to run. He could invest the money in stocks or gamble it away in a casino. He would stake it on Sabrina, the safest asset he knew of, she had convinced him of that by entrusting him with her phone number. He would call her tomorrow morning. Tomorrow morning he would be looking forward to tomorrow evening. Tomorrow afternoon he would book a flight for two days' time. Sabrina would by then have specified their destination. Hong Kong, Shanghai or Beijing. Or someplace quite else: Italy or the Caribbean, France or Switzerland. He now had to perform the trick of getting to the ground floor and out of the house as unobtrusively as he had made his way through the rooms upstairs. In the bedroom of the master of the house he had almost in passing and quite unexpectedly, of course, unearthed two credit cards. Those he rejected in favor of taking three little gold bars that had been left lying around on top of a massive chest of drawers – negligently, in the way that only the wealthy treat articles of value. This struck him as less criminal and not as dangerous as filching the credit cards, which he wouldn't have known what to do with in any case. There was bound to be a safe here as well. The master of the house had meant to put the gold bars away in it before he was distracted by a phone call or a new idea. Now Lorenz had forestalled him. He almost laughed aloud.

So much luck and lack of opposition were hard to grasp. He hadn't hesitated – he'd seized his chance, and this time it hadn't eluded him. That was why the plastic bags felt heavy and light at the same time.

Friedrich Franz Bentz would sooner or later notice his loss, but he would probably get over it more easily than he would the death of a domestic pet – not, Lorenz assumed, that the Bentzes had a pet. Not a dog, anyway. If there had been a dog, he would never have dared carry out his daring plan.

I was unafraid, he told himself before the door opened, the light came on, and he was confronted by a good-looking elderly woman. She shut the door behind her. This intrepid matron with ice-gray, piled-up hair could only be Verena Bentz. The house was obviously well insulated, because he hadn't heard her coming. She did not look particularly surprised, let alone scared.

Marina

Marina opened her handbag and felt inside. An attack of goose bumps made her shiver. What she was feeling was not leather but Amadou's skin, which her fingers were slowly and intently stroking, back and forth. Skin and leather were as soft, cool, and smooth as each other. Embedded in the memory of her fingertips was the memory of his skin. The leather was capable of reproducing it just as her fingertips were capable of remembering.

The leather exterior and lining of the handbag were like Amadou's skin, the same color, the same texture, the same consistency. They felt silky and lukewarm, with a tendency to heat up if Marina's fingers stroked the same spot for any length of time. He had given her this handbag at the end of their eleventh night, one night before the twelfth, the last night they'd spent together. The handbag, the leather, the color would always remind her of what she had missed thereafter. She would never be parted from the handbag. She would always carry it. The handbag had what it took to outlive her. She would sooner forget his voice, and what it had said, than his skin. Not his skin. Never. All that remained of his voice was its husky, muted quality, which forbade her ever to be noisy. He had left her the bag as a memento, the color and texture being no accident. Amadou was affectionate and vain, as extravagantly affectionate as extravagantly vain, but in the end a little less affectionate than vain, because he had gone away without telling her and she hadn't heard a word from him since. Without any explanation – he certainly didn't acknowledge the need for any – he had vanished into the desert that had probably sprung from her imagination alone. She had waited for a long time and was really still waiting – for what if not for him. She had waited in vain for long enough and would continue to do so, although she knew that waiting bore no fruit. She should have known when he gave her the bag. The bag was an expression of all that he was and was leaving behind. It was all he could give of himself. She should at least have guessed that it was a token of farewell when, with an artless smile, he handed it to her carelessly wrapped in gray gift-wrapping with numerous tears in it: a souvenir, his inimitable way of saying thank-you. She had initially construed the gesture, which she understood only later, as a quite normal though expensive gift. He was so different, that was all, but so completely different that it had taken her breath away – and certainly not hers alone. When he was there, and even when he wasn't. His skin was a mirror that told her the truth the longer she looked at herself in it. The truth about him, and about her, and about everything else.

The bag had been made in the Atelier Renard on the Place du Palais-Bourbon in Paris, which dozed to itself in the shade of some big eighteenth-century buildings behind the National Assembly. Proust used to stroll here, her father would have said, perhaps correctly, perhaps not, she had read as little Proust as Droste-Hülshoff. It was utterly improbable that Amadou had bought the bag there, as improbable that he had bought it at all. Those bags could not be bought anywhere. They were not on sale in any shops on any boulevards, neither in Paris nor elsewhere. He had stolen it. For him, with his slender, nimble, knowledgeable fingers, that would have been child's play. Or a habit. Or something indispensable. Everything about him differed from what one knew of other men. She would never know whether he had made off with it for herself or for another woman, after his Berber's eye had instantly recognized its value. Not knowing was less hurtful than knowing. At all events, the bag was either new or had been used so little that it looked new. Where he was now she didn't know. She didn't even know if he was still alive. All she knew was, she hadn't imagined him.

Amadou was as real as this bag. The leather looked alive, as alive as him. Her hand stroked the leather until it reached the spot where the logo was impressed, not on the outside but inside, for discretion was one of the commandments upheld by the small, woman-run, bag-maker's workshop, and upheld with a punctiliousness exceeded only by the quality of its artifacts and the prices paid for them. She had long been able to read the logo like a blind woman. Renard, the fox. The fact was, Amadou had also been a fox.

One day months later she had flown to Paris – just for a day and a night – and taken a taxi from the Gare Montparnasse straight to the National Assembly. The taxi had pulled up outside the building in which the Atelier Renard – "Sellier Maroquinier à Paris" – was situated. Outside No. 3, right next to a restaurant with a terrace on which a lot of people were sitting, mostly dark-suited men and women plus a few tourists and some local residents. The restaurant was evidently patronized at lunchtime by politicians who delivered speeches in the impressive parliament building, showering each other with insults and, in the end, voting precisely as expected: a swarm of self-opinionated bees with a handful of Japanese visibly enjoying themselves in their midst. In Paris, otherwise than in Berlin, people didn't talk about tourists, they ignored them.

Of course Amadou had stolen the bag, but certainly not from the Paris workshop, because the latter lay hidden and protected from thieves in a cool, elegant interior courtyard doubly secured by a keypad and a heavy iron door. Oleanders blossomed in a dozen massive terracotta urns, exotic plants and ivy proliferated on the windowsills. Not everyone was granted admittance. There was an intercom system, and she would be asked who she was. She would say she was interested in buying a bag. She didn't have Amadou's bag with her. They would undoubtedly have recognized it and been surprised not to remember its owner. She could have said she'd been given it as a gift. Which was true. But perhaps the bag manufacturer would recognize it as one that had been stolen from a customer. She didn't want to risk that, because she would never give the bag back.

First, however, she had sat on the restaurant terrace, impassively exposed to the gaze of men who, as expected, commenced their inspection with her crossed legs and lingered on her mouth, nose, and eyes before pretty soon returning to her legs. She ordered a coffee. She wasn't hungry despite not having eaten since breakfast. Later she might eat something sweet somewhere – she had a yen for something sweet. She could have flown to Paris more often. The restaurant was still full although it was already half past two. Newcomers kept squeezing past her at the back of the terrace, under the awning, or into the interior. She herself was sitting in full sunlight.

Having paid, she spent a while standing in front of the blue wooden door before pushing it open and going inside. Then she rang the bell and was admitted after inquiring via the intercom if she might see a few bags. "*Bien sûr, entrez! C'est juste devant vous, derrière à droite.*" The door opened and she was cordially welcomed by the woman owner, who had, she learned, taken over the business from Monsieur Renard many years ago. The likeliest scenario, alas, was that Amadou had wrenched the bag he'd given her off the arm of a woman on the street, but she was loath to think of that. That was the last thing she wanted to think of – that and the possibility that his victim might have fallen over and hurt herself. The owner and her employees were extremely friendly. Their manner toward a potential customer was anything but obsequious, let alone condescending.

"One has to feel and touch a bag," said the bag manufacturer, "and also discuss it thoroughly." Having consulted her limited knowledge of French, Marina presumed she had gotten the gist of "*sentir, toucher, palabrer.*" She could have talked about her bag for hours. She wouldn't buy another bag, she didn't need one. She discovered that hers was of goatskin and had cost around 10,000 euros.

When she had left the workshop and was crossing the courtyard, she passed two women who looked vaguely familiar. They laughed as they entered the building at the rear, but not before exchanging a few words with the owner of the workshop. They appeared to be happy people in a happy home. Actresses?

Marina took the money Melzer had given her from her bag and spread it out in front of her. She eyed it as her fingers stroked Amadou's soft, pale brown skin. Either he would come back or he wouldn't. She could hardly remember Melzer's face. Water under the bridge.

Marek

First he greedily drained the glass of beer he had so much been looking forward to, then he ordered a Moscow Mule. In a sense, this sealed the irrevocability of the decision he'd put into effect, because even if someone ran him to earth – which was unlikely – he couldn't possibly return to the concert platform. He had never played a single note in public after taking a drink.

The bar was suffused with the warmth and gloom he liked so much in bars in cities in the States. Like them, this one was snugly comforting.

It was a rambling establishment on three different levels. Customers in its various niches and alcoves were safe from inquisitive eyes without having to feel either hemmed in or excluded. Nearly half the big, central room was taken up by an oval, mahogany-colored bar counter. No bar pianist was seated at the baby grand in the corner. All the absence of dust on its lid betokened was that it was dusted daily.

Aside from the bartender, who was just bending down to get some ice, which he shoveled into a champagne bucket, none of the employees was probably older than forty and none looked older than thirty-five at most. The men far outnumbered the women, and all wore burgundy jackets.

The music issuing from invisible loudspeakers was by Diana Krall, who had only recently felt flattered to be congratulated by Olsberg on her exceptional talent as a pianist and singer. That was what she had said, at least, and he'd had no reason to doubt her sincerity. She had no need to fear any competition from him, nor to learn anything from him. That, if he remembered rightly, had been on the occasion of one of her concerts in Toronto or Montreal, where he had appeared the following day. What would she think of him when she learned of the incident in Berlin?

So now he was sitting alone in a bar, listening with his eyes shut to Diana singing "The Boulevard of Broken Dreams." Hadn't she even made a CD of Christmas carols? His thoughts strayed, her voice died away and was replaced by that of another woman, probably black. A black voice. What differentiated black voices from white? At some point he ordered another Moscow Mule. He would soon be tipsy if he went on drinking like this. His eyes sought a mirror in which to toast himself, but all they found was a few irregular gaps between countless bottles, so he raised his glass only a little and put it to his lips. He took a tiny sip. It tasted more delectable that anything he'd drunk for a long time. What was he doing here, why was he here?

He would somehow have to foot the bill for the Philharmonie's loss. It would cost him a lot of money, fifty thousand, a hundred thousand, but money did not play an important role in his life. He had no idea what lay ahead, he took only a casual interest in what was known as business. He would apologize, he was rich, he'd invested most of his money in London real estate and a Swiss bank account. London property prices had doubled, trebled, multiplied. He found it hard to recall what the prices had been fifteen years ago, and he didn't know how high they were now. There was no doubt that they had risen immeasurably. He was rich. He had gained his wealth with his hands, his memory, his talent. He would tell those who knew him the truth, even though he didn't know what it was. He would give no interviews, refuse to be coaxed out of his shell. He would entrust his attorney with the matter. His attorney would soon find out what expenses had been incurred by the promoter, the agency, and himself. Perhaps an insurance company would step in. He had taken out more than one insurance policy in his life and had never made a claim. Would they cover this business? "Cheek to Cheek," but not with Diana Krall. He recognized the pianist at once: André Previn, under whose baton he had played in Washington in the days when he still performed with orchestra. They would come to an arrangement. They would take account of the artist's nervous strain. How many concerts had Benedettti Michelangeli or Fischer-Dieskau canceled in the course of their lives? But had anyone ever stood up and walked out although the auditorium was packed, although the concertgoers were quiet as mice, although the piano wasn't out of tune, although no cellphones were ringing, no hearing aids chirping, and no one coughing or rustling silver paper? He took another sip and looked up.

Lorenz

She did something he hadn't been expecting. She put her left forefinger to her lips and extended her right hand. He was meant to shake it like a welcome visitor – that, at least, was how he interpreted the gesture. Was he a welcome visitor? Instead of screaming and calling for her husband and the police, as any other woman would probably have done, she was extending a silent welcome. What was her intention? Why was she doing this? She naturally didn't know who he was and had never seen him before, but it was easy to tell from his clothes how he had gotten in, that his route had not been that of an ordinary burglar, and that he was very probably one of the catering service employees whose reason for entering her house had been a social function that did not take place.

Her expression was amused rather than annoyed or concerned. She did not look in fear for her life. Despite her modern attire she might have hailed from another century – an impression that did not stem only from the peculiar hairdo towering above her forehead, not a strand of which had come adrift.

"You came here to rob us, and it looks as if you've already succeeded." She indicated the two plastic bags. Lorenz went weak at the knees. His throat was dry. What did she want him to say?

"Would you like to sit down?"

He couldn't get a word out, but he managed to shake his head.

"Lost your tongue?"

He searched for words and eventually said, "It wasn't planned." She waited for him to elaborate.

"I'm not a burglar or a thief, I'm a totally harmless individual. This is the very first time – nothing like this ever occurred to me before tonight. It's against my nature. At least, I thought so until now."

"You mean we encouraged you to do it? You mean it was only the surroundings we lured you into that have made you what you are, though only temporarily, am I right?" The word "surroundings" was accompanied by a gesture that clearly encompassed the whole house. "We were asking for it and we got it, eh?"

"My life is a complete..." He groped for words again. "I've..."

Verena Bentz sat down, looking thoughtful and abstracted. At length she said, "It's been a long night without any closure – dissatisfying, in that respect. On the other hand, if tonight hadn't happened I'd have been deprived of this enjoyable incident. This incident is compensating me for a pleasure cut short, and it's quite as unusual as Olsberg's exit. From my point of view, anyway, and evidently from yours as well."

"Are you going to call the police?"

"Of course not! I said this was enjoyable."

"I'll put everything back where I took it from."

"No," she said quietly. Just then she noticed the remains of the glass pelican. "Luckenwalde," she said. "That's where my family comes from. The pelican is the city's heraldic beast. One wonders how a pelican would have found its way there."

"I'd gladly replace it for you."

"My family doesn't amount to much more than these few fragments either."

But she bent down and picked up the beak. She looked at it for a while and then dropped it. It smashed like the rest of the glass bird. "A memento," she said, "but I don't feel sad. Luckenwalde was a very long time ago."

She scrutinized him.

"How old are you?"

"Thirty-eight, nearly thirty-nine."

"You don't look like a waiter."

"It's what I do, though, and not just to earn money."

"It may be how you earn your living, but you don't look as if it's enough for you."

"Yes, it is. I can lie in. I can sleep for as long as I like."

"Tonight you obviously found it isn't enough to meet all your needs."

She knew nothing. He wouldn't tell her about Sabrina. He remained silent.

"You don't really know what you want. Would you like to go now?"

Yes, he wanted to go. He nodded.

"My husband is in his bedroom already. We sleep apart. He won't emerge until tomorrow morning, he sleeps soundly thanks to his pills. Your colleagues went home long ago. Everyone else has gone to bed. No more unsuspecting guests are to be expected, it's nearly midnight. Everyone knows by now what happened tonight. The Olsberg business, I mean. I'll see you out. Ah yes, shall I call you a taxi? You can pay for it yourself. It's a long way to the nearest streetcar stop, as you know. I'm sure you won't want to walk that far."

She ordered a taxi on her cellphone. Her voice was firm, her tone resolute.

"Better wait outside the gate, I don't want the cabby ringing the doorbell. My husband might hear, or the housekeeper, whom I'm sure you met. And don't forget your bags."

Lorenz had left them on the floor. He started to say something, but she cut him short. She spoke almost gently.

"I'm not interested in their contents. I don't care what you've taken. You're welcome to put something else in." Again she made a sweeping gesture.

But Lorenz shook his head. He wasn't going bend down. "Thanks, it's nice of you, but it wouldn't be appropriate." Although the right word eluded him, his meaning was plain enough.

She picked up one of the bags and felt inside. He didn't know whether her almost inaudible "Oh!" resulted from coming across the gold bars. She fished out the wad of bills and pressed it into his hand.

"Please take this. It's a gift you can't refuse without wanting to seem extremely impolite and ungrateful. It's your payment for trusting me and not running away. You could also have hit me over the head. Theoretically, I could now be lying in a pool of my own blood. But you don't look like that. Neither like a thief nor like a waiter. More like my son, except that I don't have one, just three quarrelsome daughters. Two of them are married to lawyers and the third has just divorced. I never gathered what her husband did for a living. Maybe you know what I mean?"

No, he hadn't the remotest idea, but why should he tell her so? Anyway, she'd been speaking more to herself. Verena Bentz opened the door and escorted him out. She turned on the light and they went downstairs together to the hall, which was totally silent, she hugging the wall and he next to the banisters. Once downstairs she opened the front door and let him out. Putting a finger to her lips once more, she closed the door behind him. It was cool outside but the rain had stopped. It was like the end of a secret assignation.

Sabrina was standing at the gate. No, he was only imagining it. Or was he? The taxi would probably be a while yet.

Nico and Marek

"A beer."

The bartender's back was obscuring Marek's view of the person he'd heard clear his throat and then order a beer. When he moved aside, Marek caught sight of a young man who had sat down at the bar across from him and stared into space until he, too, looked up and recognized him. Yes, the young man undoubtedly knew who he was. He had followed him here! That was Marek's first thought. His second was that this was unlikely, he would have noticed. No one could have tailed him. He had been quicker than the others, had stood up and disappeared more swiftly. The young man gave him a broad smile. Marek smiled back. The youthful stranger looked wide-awake. What was he doing here? What was going on? His impression that the young man's lips were moving, mouthing the name Marek Olsberg, was not a delusion. After that his smile widened still more. He was pleased. They both were.

Marek nodded a mute response. He was still Olsberg, even if he wasn't playing anymore.

Moving toward one another like iron and magnet, they both rose simultaneously and sat down at their point of convergence, the narrow end of the oval counter, where they were almost face to face on their bar stools and could easily have touched. The bartender watched them without moving. He silently deposited Nico's beer in his new place, then went to Marek's old place, picked up his half-empty cocktail glass, and deposited it in his new place. Cocktail glass and beer mug clinked softly as they touched.

"You're Marek Olsberg, aren't you? Why aren't you playing, why are you here? You aren't his double, surely?"

Marek laughed.

"Perhaps I am."

"But it's only…" Nico broke off, reluctant to look at the clock. "The concert would last longer than this, any concert would. The audience goes wild when Olsberg plays, or so I've heard."

"I've just stopped playing. How did you know who I am?"

"So you aren't Olsberg's double?"

"Sometimes, maybe, but certainly not now."

Marek laughed softly. Nobody could overhear what they were talking about, not even the seemingly inattentive bartender.

"What's your name?" Marek asked with a smile.

"Nico."

"And where do we know each other from?"

"Do we know each other?"

"In some strange way."

"I know your recordings."

"How old are you?"

"Twenty-four."

"My God, so young. I could be your father."

"No, you couldn't."

Marek cocked an eyebrow.

"No?"

"What are you doing here?"

"What are *you* doing here? Aren't you a fan? Aren't you one of those who'd do anything to get hold of a ticket to hear and see me?"

"Sure. I was on my way to your concert tonight, but it didn't work out."

"Why not?"

"You know Claudius."

Marek looked surprised. "What?"

"Claudius and I were on our way to the Philharmonie when we got into a row. We were in a cab, we quarreled, and I got out somewhere."

"You and Claudius?"

"He promised to introduce me to you after the concert. I'm sure he'd have let me squeeze your hand and whisper a few words of thanks and appreciation. Then we'd have gone to the party together."

His forefinger brushed Marek's hand like a fly, so fleetingly that Marek almost believed he'd only imagined it.

"But then we quarreled and I got out and went to the movies and he went on alone to the concert." Nico made a little, derogatory gesture. His hand came to rest very close to Marek's, as if glued to the bar.

"We're always quarreling."

"So are we."

"We're incompatible. We may be too alike, the way they always say in movies, and that's why it obviously doesn't work. No idea. I think it's something else. I can't find a word for it and I don't have to. He went on to your concert by himself. Maybe he thinks I wanted to punish him. I'd have liked to hear you play. I'm here purely by chance. What a coincidence that I should meet you here, of all places. But what are you doing here?"

"Well, chatting with you, Nico. What else?"

"Would you like to know why we quarreled?"

"No, but I'd like to know why you don't call me by my first name when I call you Nico. Is it because I could be your father after all?"

"My father looks quite different. He may even be younger than you. But there's no resemblance — no, none at all. It's like we're from two different planets. Have you spoken with Claudius?"

"Today, you mean?"

"Yes."

"No, we telephone only rarely. He does his job and I do mine, we each go our own way. Everyone does what they can, and Claudius is a good agent. One of the best."

"What happened?"

"It's too long ago."

"I mean, what happened tonight?"

Marek said nothing for a long time, but instead of looking sheepishly in the air he gazed into Nico's violet eyes, which proved, on closer inspection, not to be violet at all but pale gray with a touch of feline green, not amber-colored like Claudius's, of which he had a vague recollection. They had once been as close as he now was to this recently adult young stranger whose presence simultaneously disturbed and relaxed him to such an extent that he was saying things he wouldn't have said to anyone, not even his best friends – least of all to them, in fact.

"I only know what happened, but I've no idea why. I sometimes felt I existed only while playing. I don't know whether it was bound to end, but it seems to me it did tonight. It ended well, I think. I got up and walked out."

Nico stared at him wide-eyed.

"I got up and walked out."

"What? During the recital?"

"Right in the middle of it. I knew things couldn't go on like this, it was impossible. I have to stop. If I don't, something far more terrible will happen than me simply stopping and – admittedly – offending a lot of people. I have to stop or nothing more will happen, nothing at all. How terrible that would be. It mustn't come to that. I can't explain it to you because I can't explain it to myself, nor do I have to."

"Was it during the Hammerklavier Sonata?"

"Just before the end of the great fugue."

"Wow!"

"I got up and walked out without saying a word. I hadn't intended to. It wasn't a long-cherished wish. It wasn't premeditated – nothing in my life has been less premeditated than that, even winning first prize in the Grand Concours de Budapest. Whatever people thought, they'll end by saying they were present on a great occasion, Marek Olsberg's last concert! That will far outweigh their short-lived annoyance. They'll start changing their minds tomorrow – their indignation will dissipate as quickly as it came. All that people lust after today are sensations: the fastest Chinese, the noisiest German, the smarmiest Viennese, the most excitable Frenchwoman. I'll name no names. I never name names because I know how unjust I am − because I'm considered believable and trustworthy. Tell me about yourself. You're Claudius's friend? Since when? Do you live together?"

Nico shook his head. "Neither one nor the other."

Marek put out his hand and touched Nico's shoulder without giving any thought to whether he might feel harassed. "But he hasn't simply been using you?"

"No idea. What does 'using' mean? I'm an adult, aren't I? Not very old, but not in the first flush of youth either. At all events, not a child anymore. I'm not letting myself be used, whatever that means. I know what I'm doing."

Marek let go of Nico's shoulder and stood up. He looked around for a moment and said, "I'm glad you found me here. I'm glad you came."

He walked across the room to the deserted piano, opened the lid, and sat down. For a moment it looked like the bartender was going to call out, "Hey, just a minute," but Marek's fingers were already on the keys, and everyone present instantly grasped that this customer wasn't one of the usual pains in the ass who have only to catch sight of a piano in the distance to feel they have to tinkle on it.

Marek Olsberg played Chopin's Nocturne No. 2 in E Flat Major for his new friend, about whom all he knew was his first name and that fact that he was, or had been, Claudius's friend. The look in his eyes, which did not leave Nico's face, underwent a change as he was playing, and from the very first bar the few customers present diverted their attention from what they had been doing until that moment. The bartender turned off the music system, and whoever had been singing or playing fell silent. The room that had not been designed for such music became a room in which that music ebbed and flowed, awoke and slumbered, was born and died.

The bar was pervaded by a strange unease after the last note had died away, but it soon subsided. Marek closed the piano and gave Nico a hug.

Coda

Two weeks after Olsberg's memorable last recital, which had for several days received exhaustive coverage in the international press, the Berlin Philharmonic performed under the baton of Sir Simon Rattle. The concert opened with Joseph Haydn's "The Clock" Symphony and ended with Gustav Mahler's Symphony No. 1, "The Titan." Few would have noticed that night if someone had stood up and left the concert hall saying, "That's that."

People continued to discuss the scandalous incident for longer than two weeks, and many who had only heard tell of it behaved as if they had been present at the time.

#

"It would make a short story," Solveig said a few weeks later, when she was attending a recital of piano duets. If one of the performers had stood up that night, the other would have been bound to restrain them, so no repetition of the incident was to be feared.

"But who'd write it?" Esther retorted almost tartly, her thoughts elsewhere. She'd always had the impression that Solveig hadn't a clue about literature, even though she occasionally claimed to have just read this or that book under discussion.

"I mean, what would it be about? Someone stops playing, gets up, and walks out. What kind of story is that? That's what he said, wasn't it? That's that?"

Solveig shrugged her shoulders and concentrated on the music, which would steer her thoughts in a different direction.

#

The pianists were playing on two pianos, so the blind piano tuner Dr. Hiller would have more work than two weeks ago, when Marek Olsberg had left the concert platform and disappeared from public life forever. He was as usual sitting up in Block C, in the last row on the right.

Acknowledgments

I owe a great debt of gratitude to my distinguished accompanists, the pianists Yaara Tal and Andreas Groethuysen, who jointly helped me on my way through the pianistic jungle. I am equally grateful to Andreas Wittmann, oboist of the Berlin Philharmonic, who brought light into the darkness of my ignorance of the Philharmonie concert hall, both backstage and below-stage. I should also like to thank Brigitte Montaut, owner of the Atelier Renard in Paris, for permitting me to feel all kinds of leather and generously sharing her professional knowledge with me. Without my invisible assistants, this book would be poorer in many respects.

I should also like to express my gratitude to the UBS Kulturstiftung, the Fondation Jan Michalski, and the Landis & Gyr Stiftung for lending me financial support and enabling me to spend six months in Berlin.

Lightning Source UK Ltd.
Milton Keynes UK
UKOW03f1341070914

238192UK00001B/5/P